By Jud
Rule

Commander James Bondage

By Judicial Decree 13
Rules of Evidence

SILVER MOON BOOKS

Introduction

Welcome, Faithful Readers, to the 13th, and in all probability, final story in the By Judicial Decree series. Some of you may have noted that characters in recent books in the series have been wondering if Caine is getting a little long in the tooth to continue the strenuous exercise required by his hobby of slave training, and upon mature consideration, I am forced to agree. So rather than risk losing him to a stroke or heart attack caused by a session of over-enthusiastic erotic activities wit one of his lovely playthings, I am going to retire the old warhorse.

Those of my Faithful Readers who are already familiar with the novels in this series (which I assume is most of you,) will note that this story does not follow the usual pattern, but is different in a number of ways which you will have to discover for yourselves. However, I trust that I have included sufficient quantities of the themes and characters from previous volumes that attracted you to these stories originally. Only time (and book sales) will tell if I was right.

But enough of this stalling. It is high time for me to step aside, and introduce you to the charming sociopath and wireless celebrity, Betty Carroll, and her companion in bondage, the lovely, young, and perplexing Halli Fairbourne.

Warmest regards,

Commander James Bondage

Preface

It is only by an accident of history that we no longer observe the ancient Roman custom of judicial enslavement for debt or as a penalty for a criminal conviction. But what if history had taken a different path? Modern physics teaches that there are an infinite number of universes, and therefore an infinite number of Earths, some so similar as to be indistinguishable from our own, others so different as to be unrecognizable. Among the infinite number of possibilities then, there are an infinite number of Earths where history did go a different way than ours. Therefore, there must exist somewhere Earths in which the old Roman laws are followed, and slavery is still on the books. This story is set in one of those histories.

Chapter One: Fallen

She was seated astride a wooden horse, a wedge mounted on four legs. It was a most uncomfortable seat, and she would have gladly dismounted, if that had been possible. However, for several very good reasons, she could not. For one, there were leather cuffs around her ankles attached by short chains to 1/2 inch metal bolts sunk in the floor. There was sufficient slack in these ankle chains to allow her to go up on her toes, but they permitted no movement beyond that. So she was just barely able to raise herself clear of the base of the 3-inch long plastic probe attached to the top of the horse that was inserted in her rectum, and she was doing so to the best of her ability. She had a strong incentive for standing *en pointe*, because while the probe was only perhaps an inch in diameter, the base was covered with hard plastic carbuncles that soon felt like the spines of a saguaro cactus on the sensitive tissues of her colon.

It seemed that her new owner was worried that she might not be uncomfortable enough, so he had put considerable ingenuity into ensuring against this possibility. In addition to everything else, her arms were pressed together behind her back in a single glove so tight that it made her elbows touch and forced her shoulders together until her shoulder blades met. This in turn made her thrust her chest out dramatically, presenting her not overly large, but extremely shapely breasts, in a spectacular display. They projected outward as if she was

9

offering them up to the next person to enter the room, which was not coincidentally, exactly what the person who had designed this bondage had in mind.

The single glove alone placed an increasingly painful strain on her arms, shoulders, and back, but once again, her tormentor had not settled for the merely painful, when he could shoot for agonizing. Instead of her compressed, aching arms being allowed to drop down to her back, a cord had been run through a ring at the end of the glove, then drawn up until her arms were higher than her head.

The cord placed another kind of pressure on her shoulder joints, and the only way to relieve it was to bend forward at the waist. This of course made her press her pelvis down on the wedge that formed the top of the horse, making the steel cleave more deeply into her sex, while at the same time, the bumpy anal probe was driven further up her rear orifice. She was presented with a dilemma: if she sat up as straight as possible and stood on her toes, she could keep most of her weight off the wedge cutting her vulva and the dildo buried inside her rectum, but in that position, the pressure on her upper arms and shoulders quickly became unendurable, and she was obliged to bend forward once more, subjecting her private places to renewed torment.

Eventually, the process of shifting from the shoulder-cracking position to the ass-and-pussy splitting one became more or less automatic. Her body cycled from one to the other in a vain search for relief without any need for conscious thought on her part. The pain too became such a constant companion that, like the position of her body, it no longer demanded her full attention. This was unfortunate in one respect, as it left her free to brood over the recent disastrous decisions she had made that had landed her here.

She had fallen from a high place (she had not been from the nobility perhaps, but she had become a national wireless celebrity, which was something,) into slavery, and what was to her mind, the lowest, most degrading imaginable form of slavery, at that. She had not been purchased as a domestic, a housemaid assigned to dusting off mantles in some mansion, nor as a kitchen drudge, washing pots and peeling potatoes, nor even a farmhand, lugging around a basket full of apples or picking cotton all day in the hot sun. Any of these jobs would have, in her opinion, been far better than what actually awaited her, for she was the chattel of a man who intended to train and use her as a pleasure slave. While the job of a fuck-toy might be less physically demanding than twelve hours in the field hauling around a 50-pound sack of cotton, she nonetheless considered the former less desirable than even the most exhausting physical labor. As far as she was concerned, males were subhuman, perverted animals, with what tiny brains they possessed stored in their pants, whose one goal was to slake their primitive urges on women in general, and her in particular. She had learned to hide her true feelings, and to use their mindless lust to manipulate males, while managing to avoid their repulsive

11

embraces...until now. But like every other good thing in her life, that was about to come to an end.

Betty, she told herself, *you really landed yourself in the shit this time*. She idly wondered what prison life was like and decided that, in retrospect, a few years behind bars would not have been so bad. *It would have to be better than this, anyway*, she concluded. There was more truth in this thought than she knew, for as yet, she had not yet experienced the reality of being a pleasure slave in *this* house.

She shifted on the horse again, winced briefly at the sharp pain the movement set off in her pussy and anus, then returned to castigating herself for the overweening arrogance that had brought her here, mounted like a display mannequin in the window of a sex shop. *You thought you could outsmart everybody: the jury, the judge, your lawyer, and that little prosecutor bastard, too*, she told herself, *but the only one you outsmarted was yourself. You're a fucking idiot, Betty. You deserve to be a fuck-toy. You're too stupid for anything else. You're too stupid to live. You ought to ...*

This brutal self-appraisal was interrupted by the sound of creaking hinges. She had heard that sound twice before, the first time when the door to the room was opened, just before she was taken inside by her escorts. The second time was after they had finished mounting her on this obscene steed, when the two sullen house servants left there alone in the dark, slamming the door shut behind them.

She heard the slap of shoe leather on the cement floor, the sound growing louder as the new arrival approached. She automatically tried to ask who was there, momentarily forgetting that the hard rubber ball wedged behind her teeth precluded intelligible speech. All she got out around the obstruction was an inscrutable, "Ooh uhh ahh?"

He heard a sharp *crack*, and an instant later, something traced a burning line of agony diagonally down her back from the left shoulder blade to the right hip. She screamed, producing an unimpressive, low, muffled sound, and lurched forward, causing a crunching noise to come from her shoulders. She heard the voice of her new owner. "It is my understanding that you need some smarts to run a successful con operation," he said, "but you seem a little too slow on the uptake for anything as complicated as that. Is it possible that you have already forgotten Rule Number One? Well, I'll repeat it for you: slaves don't speak without permission."

She shrieked at the top of her lungs again, with the same unsatisfactory result, when the whip completed a crimson "X" across the whiteness of her back, with a stroke from her right scapula to her left hip. Once again, the stroke made her hop involuntarily in the air, with agonizing consequences for her bruised and tender private regions when she landed. The metal wedge was particularly noticeable by the way it cleaved her vulva so viciously that she imagined it was cutting her in two. Then she dropped heavily on the base of the anal dildo, receiving the full sensation of the knobby surface all at once on the delicate tissues of her colon. She threw back her head and howled in distress, like a she-wolf baying at the moon.

After the next stroke raised a welt horizontally across her back, she opened her mouth even wider than the ball jammed in behind her front teeth, something she had not believed was possible. This allowed the escape of an ear-piercing shriek, comparable in volume to a police siren. She involuntarily flung herself sharply forward, ramming her clitoris sharply down on the metal wedge, then automatically rebounded, throwing herself back just as violently. The latter movement felt as if she had just dislocated both shoulders. While she was thus contorting in agony, her invisible assailant exchanged the whip for a rubber truncheon. When she finally settled down again, he struck her with this instrument on her left breast. The blow was so hard that the shaft of the club momentarily sank out of sight in the flesh.

The next blow landed on her solar plexus, driving all the air out of her lungs and turning her midsection to stone. She shook her head, grimaced from the sudden sunburst of pain, then concentrated as she had never concentrated before, trying to start breathing again. After a subjective lifetime in Hell, her respiratory system began to function again, and she was able to draw in a ragged breath.

Time passed, something between fifteen minutes and eternity, she estimated, and he spoke again. His voice was pitched so low that she could barely make out his words over the sounds of her own panting.

"You are here because you murdered a man, an old friend of yours," he said, in a steady baritone. "So in a sense, I have been appointed by fate to avenge his death; certainly, no-one else will, because no-one really cared about him. But I didn't tell Quentin to buy you and bring you here to punish as you deserve for your crime, nor to lay the ghost of the late, unlamented Lars Forsberg." He paused to open the catch of the strap at the back of her head, then held out his hand to accept the saliva-covered ball-gag, when she pushed it out of her mouth with her tongue.

She expected him to continue in this vein, but instead, he said, "Come on, let's get you down from there," then knelt on the floor to release the straps on her ankles and unhook the single glove from the overhead bar, a blessed relief for her aching shoulders. She felt strong hands lifting her from the horse until, the long dildo popped out of her burning rectum (*Thank the gods*, she thought.) After he carefully set her bare feet on the cold cement floor, she sighed, and said, "Thank you. I'd almost forgotten how much it hurt to sit on that thing."

From behind, he said, "I think you'll find that your gratitude is premature." As he said this, he passed a noose around her long neck and pulled the knot firmly up against the base of her skull. The noose was at the end of a spool of coated wire that descended from an overhead drum. An instant after he had cinched up the noose, she heard the low hum of the electric motor, as the cylinder turned to take up the slack. Almost immediately after that, she felt the wire cut into her neck at the base of her jaw, drawing her relentlessly higher, first to the balls of her feet, then to her toes. For a moment she thought that he had decided to finish her then and there. But before her airway was completely closed off, he stopped the cylinder.

She found that it was possible to breathe, but only as long as she kept her head tilted up and tipped to one side, and remained on her toes. She strained to stand perfectly still, as even the smallest movement made the noose tighter. She could hear the air whistling through her constricted trachea, while gray cloud seemed to form around her brain, a sign of increasing asphyxiation.

"So why did I send Quentin up to the prison to buy you?" He asked, resuming his earlier remarks. She hoped that this question was rhetorical, as she was incapable of speech at that moment, and if he expected an answer from her, he was bound to be disappointed. Evidently, this was the case. Rather than demanding a response, he placed one hand high up on the inside of her thigh, and said, "I did it for the obvious reason: I was ready to break in a new bed slave, and I thought you would make a good one. But you probably guessed that already, didn't you?"

His hand slid up to cup the furry delta of her sex, and she shuddered. "Hmm," he said, "we'll have to trim back this jungle. I'll schedule a plucking session for you...assuming you're around long enough to make it necessary, that is."

One finger worked its way past her lower lips into her cleft, and she strained her legs, feet, and

16

toes to the absolute limit to get away from it. "However, since you don't seem very interested in the line of work I had intended you for, perhaps depilation won't be necessary," he remarked, taking his hand away and allowing her to sink back down a little to relieve the strain on her calves and ankles. "Possibly you have an aversion to sex, or men, or you simply don't like taking orders. I suppose it might be any of a hundred things. It really doesn't matter. Now, I am not an unreasonable man, despite the stories may have heard about me, so I will offer you an alternative to this unpleasant duty, if that is your desire. How does that sound?"

She thought about this as carefully as she could, considering that her brain was clouded and confused by a shortage of oxygen. On one hand, she would rather be almost anything but a fuck-toy; but on the other, she knew there had to be a catch. Masters did not *ask* what their slaves wanted; they *told* their slaves what the master wanted.

She started to shake her head, then stopped immediately when she realized that the movement made the wire dig deeper into her flesh. She concluded that the safest thing to do was to make no commitment until he explained exactly what this "alternative" was. "I...don't...," she managed to croak. "...know." She gasped for air after uttering these few words.

He pressed closer behind, drawing her nude body up against himself, so that she could feel the lump in his pants and the rough wool of his tweed jacket against her skin, while his hands reached around to gather in her breasts. "A prudent answer," he said approvingly. "At this point, you lack sufficient information to make an intelligent decision." As he said this, his hands supported her firm mounds from below, and his fingers stretched out to take control of her nipples. He tugged and twirled the brown knobs in silence for a while.

"At least you have the physical equipment for a pleasure slave," he remarked, seemingly changing the subject. "Your tits are pretty good." She wondered if he expected her to become sexually aroused when he handled her, and what his reaction would be when she responded only with disgust. Would that enrage him enough to push him over the top, and he would finish the job he had begun, lifting her by the neck from her tenuous contact with the ground, then stand back to watch her dance on the air until she stopped moving? She wondered what it would feel like to die, and what, if anything, would come afterward.

"I suppose I will have to provide more details before you can tell me your decision," he said, resuming the earlier topic. "If you're determined not to be a sex toy, you could choose to be hanged by the neck until you were dead." He paused, absent-mindedly twirling her now-stiff nipples in his fingers. "Of course, I wouldn't do it all at once; you were, after all, a moderately expensive acquisition, and I want to get my money's worth, one way or another," he went on, as if he was discussing whether to give an old toaster away to charity or just throw it away, instead of strangling a human being to death. "So, I'd certainly take my time about it, and naturally, I would give you a good going-

18

away fuck…several, I should think. So, now that you know your options, what do you say?"

She had been listening with growing horror to his calm discussion of her demise, and by the time he asked this question, she knew one thing with absolute certainty: she did not want to die, particularly not in the manner he was suggesting. She was ready to surrender to him, ready to obey him, to say and do whatever he asked, rather than that. She opened her mouth and drew in a noisy breath through her constricted throat in preparation for saying that she wanted to be his fuck-slave. But before she could do more than croak, "I…," he pushed the button controlling the overhead cylinder, and the remaining words were caught in her throat by the contracting noose. Her feet lost contact with the floor, and she dangled by her neck, kicking and twisting, frantic with terror.

"You may find this preview helpful in making up your mind," he said, his words seeming to come from far away. Iron bands formed around her heaving chest and the pressure inside her skull increased until she thought her eyes might shoot out of their sockets like missiles. "As much as we imagine that we know about something from books or seeing it in movies," he went on, seemingly oblivious to her increasingly desperate struggles, "nothing can prepare you for the real thing. Don't you agree?"

She did not, but neither did she disagree. Her response, if indeed it *was* a response, was a sort of bubbling, gargling sound that might have meant anything. In any event, she was too busy trying to

19

stay alive to make small talk. She was not particularly devout (in point of fact, she was the next thing to an atheist,) but she found herself praying for the first time since her childhood. *"Eir the merciful, I beg you for the gift of death,"* she thought, rolling her eyes up in the general direction of Valhalla. Her throat had closed completely, and her chest now felt as if it was being crushed like a junked car in a compactor. Finally, the agony lessened and her entire body began to relax when carbon dioxide instead of oxygen filled the blood in her brain. At long last, death began to wrap her in a warm, soft blanket, and the world faded to black.

But it was this was not the end. Her owner knew his business, and whatever his plans for her future might be, he was not about to let this lovely new slave expire so quickly. To her intense regret, the pain of life, which she had thought she had left behind forever, returned. She found herself bound to the cement floor on her hands and knees after she was brought screaming back to life by a deluge of ice-cold water.

"Ah! Ah! It's *cold*!!!" she howled. "*Stop*! No more, please!" A moment later, she heard a faucet handle squeak, and the shower ceased. "Thank…you," she panted.

"You're welcome," he responded amiably, laying aside the hose he had been using. "Now that you're back in the land of the living, and you've had a chance to investigate your options, perhaps you will tell me your preference."

My first *choice would be the President's Suite at the Kingsport International, but I would settle for anywhere else in the universe but here,* she thought. *Since that's not on the table, however ...* "Slave..." she blurted out between pants, then repeated, "...*your* slave, ..." She took a deep breath, looked up at him, and finished, "I want... to be your... bed-slave, Master," she puffed.

He nodded. "Very good," he said. "Now, I have to determine if you're qualified for the position." She stared at him in dismay. It seemed that her abject surrender wasn't enough; she had to...to *what*? Be interviewed for the highly sought-after position of fuck-doll? Explain why she wanted to work for him and tell him where she hoped to be in the company in five years? Describe how, ever since she could remember, she had longed to be the sex toy of a wealthy sadist? If that was what he had in mind, the all-day hanging option was starting to look much better.

Fortunately, when referred to "qualifications," he was talking about her physical attributes only. He began by drying her gleaming sweat-covered nudity with a towel, spending (in her opinion,) an inordinate length of time on her nipples and vulva. Then he knelt behind her, took her nipples in his fingers, and massaged some kind of cream or ointment into them. After a minute or so of being twirled between his fingers, her nipples stiffened again. This time, they felt even harder than they had before, and they were *much* more sensitive. They were so sensitive, in fact, that her entire body quivered each time he flicked one of the brown knobs with his fingernail. She had not known her

21

nipples were even capable of producing such a powerful sensation.

"Oh! Oh!" she gasped, as he casually batted the rubbery knobs back and forth. "What did you do...do to me?"

"Oh, nothing much," he answered. "I just rubbed some contact aphrodisiac into your tits, to help get you in the mood. How does this feel?" He pinched the swollen buttons of flesh lightly in his nails and gave them a few gentle tugs.

Her body moved in response to the tugs, and without intending to, she found herself saying, "G-good...it feels *good*." She bit her tongue just in time to stop herself from asking him to squeeze a bit harder.

He released her breasts and said, "Let's see how we're coming along down here." Hearing this, she automatically started to close her legs, then recalled the noose was still around her throat and thought better of it.

But to Caine, her defiance, as demonstrated by the attempt to deny him access to any part of her body, even if unsuccessful, was equivalent to the completed act. Rather than explain this concept verbally, he communicated it in a non-verbal way that could not easily be misunderstood. He rose, picked a paddle from a rack on the wall, and without further ado, slammed the inch-thick slab of leather into her buttocks, reproducing the geometric pattern on the face of the paddle in red on her pale, round bottom cheeks. Ignoring her shrieks of "No!" he went on to mercilessly pummel her with his ferocious weapon, accompanying the beating with a lecture.

She could only intermittently make out what he was saying, during the brief intervals between screams when she was inhaling, but she was in too much pain for his words to register at the time.

Then, suddenly, he stopped, and said, "Make up your mind, cunt; I don't have all day to fool around with you. If you are going to be *my* fuck-toy, I require a 100% commitment. If you can't give me that, let's not waste any more time. I'll string you back up, and we can spend the rest of today and all day tomorrow ..."

"*Fuck*...fuck-toy!" She had just at this moment regained the ability to speak, although she was breathing so hard that complete sentences were still not possible. Between gasps, she managed to force out, "Your...fuck...toy! I'm c-committed. All...all I want is...to serve you..., Master. Please... let me," she puffed.

"That's what I thought," he said. He reached down to the junction of her thighs and commanded, "Open up." This time, there was not even a suggestion of resistance when his fingers invaded her pussy to spread the cool, greasy salve that he had used on her nipples on her clitoris and inner lips.

If the aphrodisiac had a remarkable effect on her nipples, what it did to her clit was nothing short of astounding. Somehow, without being aware of how or when she had started, she was rolling her hips like a belly dancer on meth and making low, throat-bound moans of passion each time he

23

squeezed or twirled her love button in his fingers. In what seemed to her like no time at all, she was on the brink of a colossal orgasm. She turned her head back toward him, and begged "Please Master, won't you rub me a little *harder*? I'm so *close*."

"You certainly are," he agreed, as he took his fingers, now well coated with her cream, out of her slot. She gasped. "But you're forgetting something," he said. "As a fuck-toy, your role is not to get *your* jollies; it's for you to make sure I get mine. Understood?" He hit her with the paddle again, and she screamed.

"*Eeeeee...*, y-yes... *fuck*, that hurt!... I understand, yes!" she bellowed. "Please don't hit me with that again, I beg you."

"Don't give me a reason to," he returned. "Now get that ass up!" He touched the purple and scarlet flesh of her hindquarters lightly with the paddle, and she strained to obey, extending her legs as far as she could, until the sinews stood out from the muscles of her thighs like cables, and her shapely buttocks were provocatively displayed.

"Better," he conceded grudgingly. His fingers resumed their activities inside her cleft, and her hips almost immediately took up where they had left off, launching into an impromptu, involuntary, and quite uninhibited, version of a hula. She was again rapidly building to a volcanic climax, and she knew she would not be able to control herself when it happened.

As if he was reading her mind, he said, "If you come without permission, I will punish you

24

severely. My cunts come only when I permit it, and not before."

Right, she thought resentfully. *So why the fuck are you playing with my clit like that*? Aloud, she said "Yes, Master," as submissively as possible.

"Don't move," he warned again.

"Yes, Mast-..." she began, then shrieked in pain and surprise, "Ahh! What are you *doing*?" She very nearly flung herself forward to escape when she felt two greasy fingers thrust into her anus. It took all her willpower to remain in position. "*Stop* it..." she shouted, then recalling where she was, and the way she had been choking out her life just a few minutes earlier, paused and added, "...*please*, Master. It...*ugh*!...hurts!"

"Do you really think so?" he inquired interestedly. "In that case, I predict that will experience a difficult period of adjustment, my girl, because you will learn to accommodate much bigger objects than my fingers in your tight little ass if you want to be a pleasure slave in my house. Ass-fucking is a basic skill I require all my fuck-slaves to master." As he spoke, his fingers stretched her sore narrow back passage, heedless of her groans and pleas for mercy.

The two fingers were joined by a third, all of them plunging violently in and out, knuckle-deep in the narrow orifice, and twisting vigorously in half-circles. Although she did her best not to stir, she could not prevent her lower body from being drawn this way and that by his invading digits.

Perhaps it was the sinuous motion of her hips, the way she begged for mercy, or the exaggerated posture of her nude loveliness, but whatever the reason, Caine suddenly realized that he was as aroused as he had ever been in his life. He moved his fingers from her anus to her pussy, replacing them with the head of his stiff organ. "Keep that ass up!" he snapped, pressing the fat head of his cock against the trembling slave's rear orifice. The little ring of tissue automatically shrank in self-defense, but she knew that no matter how hard she squeezed, she would not be able to keep him out for very long. When she felt the overtaxed ring start to give way, she screamed...

Chapter Two: Shadow of the Past

It wasn't supposed to happen this way, she thought, as she mixed a drink for her uninvited visitor. The latter was sitting at his ease on her sofa, smirking complacently, as if he was her guest, rather than an intruder. "Here you are, Lars," she said. Ice cubes clinked in the cut glass tumbler as she handed him the drink. "Aquavit on the rocks, with a splash; I hope I remembered it right."

Lars took a sip, swallowed, then smiled in evident satisfaction. "I don't see why you wouldn't remember," he said. "After all, it hasn't been that long since you left me and went on the wireless, to become the favorite teacher of every little brat in the WP, while I..." he paused, and the smile disappeared, "...got a time-out from the State, and had to go stand in the corner for 5 to 10... four years, three months and 26 days, with time off for good behavior, to be exact. I think you definitely got the better of the deal, don't you, Greta?"

She winced. "I'm not Greta; not any more. You know that Lars," she answered earnestly. "It's Betty Carroll, Miss Betty, the schoolteacher, now. Greta Lundberg doesn't exist anymore. She's been forgotten, along with the foolish decisions she made, and all the people who ..." She stopped short.

"...who ever knew her, including me, or should I say, *especially* me?" Lars finished for her. He banged his glass down on the end table next to the sofa, his face darkening in anger. "Is that what you were going to say? But it wasn't so easy for me to

27

forget, *Greta*," he said, emphasizing her name. "There wasn't a whole lot other than memories to keep me occupied all those years in prison. And guess what? I remember everything we did together back in the old days, every single minute of it, just as clearly as if it happened yesterday. What I remember most of all is what happened after we were arrested. You turned your back on me and pretended you hardly knew me. You shouldn't have done that Greta, not to your partner."

He shook his head as if he was deeply disappointed in her. "Maybe when you forgot all those things, you also forgot who found you at the bus station, a runaway without a copper half-penny in your pocket, and who taught you how to survive on the street. In case you did forget, that was me," He continued. "Where do you think you would be now if I hadn't taken you under my wing? I'll tell you: you'd be another cheap hooker on some slimy pimp's string, a drug addict or alky, looking like death warmed over by the time you were 25. That's the truth, and you know it as well as I do. I saved you; I was your friend, the only one you had in the world, the one person you could count on. But then, what are friends for, if you can't throw them under the bus when you need to?" He finished bitterly.

"It wasn't like that, Lars. You know it wasn't," she said, speaking softly and trying to calm him down before the situation turned violent. "I had no control over how the cops handled my case. The DA sent me to juvenile court because I was only 17 years old, and not a legal adult. I had no say in the matter. Did you forget *that* little detail? Anyway, what was I supposed to have done for you? Would you have felt better, if they had sent *me* upstate along with you?" She now brought her superb ability to mimic real human emotions into play, a trick that she had perfected by manipulating Lars, and later used on many other men. "You just *have* to believe me, Lars: when I heard what happened to you, it almost made me sick. I felt so terrible that I wanted to kill myself. I still feel responsible in some way, even though it doesn't make any sense, because there was really nothing I…"

"Yeah, yeah, I'm sure you had a real tough time," he cut in sarcastically. "But that's all beer under the bridge now. Just to prove there's no hard feelings, I'm going to give you a chance to unload all the guilt over me that's been bothering you for so long. What do they say, 'Let the dead past bury its dead,' something like that? Let's do that: forget about the past, and talk about our future together."

Together? She repeated mentally. *I don't know about you, old boy, but I don't see* you *anywhere in my future,* she thought. "I have a better idea, Lars. Why don't you just cut out the crap, and tell me why you came here," she said, dropping the unsuccessful dramatics, and adopting a brisk, businesslike demeanor, "so I can get back to my work, and you can get back to…" she paused, then continued, "…whatever it is you do. If it'll get you out of my office and on your way elsewhere any faster, I'll fix you up with a small grubstake. I don't have a lot of cash at the moment, but I should have more than enough for a couple of days eating money and a train ticket to someplace far from away from here, where you can get a fresh start, and I can get on with my life." She opened the handbag on her desk and began to dig through it, searching for her wallet.

"As it happens, I the rest of the day free," Lars told her. "At the moment I'm between engagements, but I expect that to change shortly. In fact, I have a hunch somebody is going to offer me a job very soon, today, even. Not only that, but that same hunch tells me this job will be a high-level executive position with full benefits, a very nice starting salary, and a healthy percentage of a profitable business. And do you know *who* is going to offer me this swell job? C'mon, guess," he urged. He waited, watching as she stopped pawing through her bag and looked up at him, but she did not hazard an answer.

"*You*," he said, pointing, "that's who. That's right, you, Greta Lungren, a.k.a. Betty Carroll, are about to bring me aboard your company, today. I'm going to be your new…, oh, I don't know… the title doesn't really matter…, it could be vice-president for public relations, or maybe executive producer, if you like the way that sounds better. Actually, I'll be more a partner than an employee. Whatever the title, the main thing is that from now on, I'll be getting half the take from your books, wireless program, personal appearances, toys, clothes, and all the rest of your branded Wireless Schoolroom junk."

Whatever else he was, Lars Forsberg was not a fool, Greta knew. He would not have made such outrageous demands if he wasn't confident that he had something to back them up, and she had a pretty good idea of what it was. The thought pumped adrenalin into her veins, made her pulse race and her jaw muscles twitch. *Stay calm, Betty*, she told herself, as her always volatile temper threatened to boil over.

She drew in a deep breath before she answered When she finally did speak, she forced herself to do so slowly and evenly, although what she *really* wanted to do was dive across the desk, wrap her hands around his throat, and squeeze until his eyeballs popped out of his head. "You must have been smoking some pretty strong stuff, if you think I'm stupid enough to hire you to clean my toilets, let alone turn half my business over to you, Lars. It sounds like those years in the pen did something to your mind. At the moment, I don't have an opening for a small-time grifter who can't be trusted with a burn-out matchstick, but if you leave your name and the address of your current flophouse with my receptionist on your way out, I'll let you know, when something comes up that fits your resume," she sneered. "Now why don't you forget about whatever dope fantasy sent you here, and beat it before call Security and have you tossed out on your ear? And when you leave, I suggest you start seeing a good head-candler right away, before your delusions get you into serious trouble. Or maybe you should just crawl back down whatever hole you popped out of and pull it in after you. I don't really care where you go or what you do, just as long as do it someplace else. I'd feel terrible if I had to report you to the cops: why you might end up back in stir, and make me feel guilty all over again."

Surprisingly, Lars responded to this threat with a good-natured grin. "Oh, I think *that* would be a mistake, Greta," he said. "If you insist on kicking me out, I'll have to go peddle my story to the newspapers, or a big, national magazine, or maybe the newsreels, whichever one makes the best offer. I have some very exciting stuff to give them, you know. It's all about the shady past of a certain celebrity schoolteacher. What do you suppose all the little kiddies will think when they hear that sweet, innocent Miss Betty was the bait in an old-fashioned badger game before she became a fake schoolteacher? And what will their parents tell them, when their toddlers ask what you were doing in bed with those men in the pictures, or what you and that poor businessman were doing together between the sheets, or why that fellow with the camera broke into your hotel room to take the pictures? They might even wonder why the men suddenly emptied their wallets and gave you all the money in their wallets after they saw your ID card and found out you were jailbait."

Her suspicions were confirmed: this was exactly what she had feared. Nonetheless, she was not the kind to roll over without a fight, and being threatened only made her more determined. "Right, Lars," she said with a show of confidence that she did not feel, "as if anyone in his right mind would believe the word of a reprobate like you."

She was even more disturbed when he responded with a bark of laughter. "Ha! You do that

32

very well, kid," he admitted. "You're a natural; no wonder you made it in show biz. Of course, I wouldn't expect anybody to take *my* word over yours, especially such a shocking story about the oh-so-wholesome Miss Betty. That's why I put together so much evidence: police reports, newspaper articles, court papers, with all the names, dates and places...oh, and these."

He reached into the inside pocket of his overcoat and pulled out a fat buff envelope. He tossed the envelope onto her desk. It was not sealed, and a half-dozen photographs spilled out. "You didn't think I told you where *all* the copies of my pictures were stashed away, did you, Greta? It's a hard, hard world out there. and even though I trusted you at the time, I knew there might come a time when we might not be... on the best of terms any longer, let's just say. That's why I squirreled this stuff away for a rainy day, and what do you know?..." he held out his hand as if testing for rain, and pretended to study the sky, "...it looks like a regular frog-strangler out there. Take a look," he suggested, nodding at the envelope. "There are some great shots of you in that lace nighty. You were one hot piece of ass back in those days...almost as hot as you are now," he continued, undressing her with his eyes and running his tongue over his lips.

She glanced down momentarily at the envelope, then back at Lars. She didn't need to examine the photographs; she knew exactly what they showed, without having to look. She glared at Lars, her lips drawn back in an animal-like snarl. For the first time in her memory, she could not think of anything to say. Her mind was empty of rational thought, which had been driven out by the red fog of rage.

"I'll give you a day or two for you to fix up my office...by the way, I'll need a corner office, a *big* one, with a decent view," Lars continued, as if the matter was now settled, "...but there's no rush about that. I can make do this one until you get my new digs ready. Oh, there is one other thing I haven't mentioned yet."

His smile made her want to smash his teeth down his throat, but she remained frozen in place, her hands balled in fists. "I'm sure you didn't forget *everything*." He went on, his tone growing more serious. "You must remember the cock-teasing games you used to play on me, when would shake your little under-age ass at me, run your hands over my crotch, then step back and laugh. You couldn't have forgotten what you did whenever I reacted exactly the way any other man would have. Just in case, I remind you: you said if I laid a finger on you, you'd have me arrested for rape. I'll lay any odds you name that you remember *that* just as well as I do, *bitch*."

By the time he spat out the final word, his face was red, his features tight with anger. He paused a moment to regain his composure, then continued in a lighter tone, "Well you're legal now, you little cockteasing slut, and you're going show me *exactly* how sorry you are about how you treated me back then. You're going to lay down on your back and spread your legs for me, and you're going to do exactly what I tell you to do, and you'll do it

34

whenever I want." He smiled again. "How's that sound, Greta?"

This new demand spurred the temporarily paralyzed Greta back to life. "No," she said, shaking her head. The thought of his grubby fingers handling her was so repulsive that it made her want to vomit. "*No*," she repeated, in a tone that wiped the smug expression off his face. She yanked open the center drawer of her desk and pulled out a small silver revolver.

Lars suddenly turned as pale as a ghost. "Aw, come on, Greta, don't be like that. I wasn't really going to do anything like that. I was just kidding around," he wheedled, as he moved closer to her, with his open hands held out placatingly and his eyes fixed on the gun. "You know what a kidder old Lars is. Now, why don't you just give me that gun, before somebody gets ...*hey*!"

"*No*!" she said, for the third time. She squeezed the trigger, firing, again and again, watching red flowers bloom on his white shirt. She continued to pull the trigger long after all eight rounds had been expended, hearing the hammer click a half-dozen times on empty chambers after Lars's body was sprawled across the sofa, his dead eyes staring at the ceiling. She was still standing behind her desk holding the gun, when her secretary burst into her office and cried, "Miss Carroll, what ..." Then seeing a bloody corpse draped across the sofa in a grotesque posture of death, she shrieked, "Odin above!"

***

35

"They're offering you a deal," Rolf Gunderman said, reaching down under the table to his briefcase and taking out a sheaf of papers, "a damn good one, too, considering the evidence. You'd be a fool not to take it." He slid the papers across the table to his client.

Greta plucked the top sheet from the stack, holding it arm's length as if the plea offer was a dead mouse. "A good deal?" She repeated doubtfully after she scanned the first paragraph. "I'm supposed to plead guilty to voluntary manslaughter. *That*'s a good deal? What kind of time would I be looking at?"

"The State's Attorney has agreed to ask for a mitigated sentence," the lawyer said. "That's what makes it a good deal. The mitigated range for voluntary manslaughter is only 7 ½ to 15, and with credit for time served, you would be eligible for parole even before you finished the minimum."

"I could get out less than 7 ½ months?" Greta asked, now more favorably inclined to the plea offer. "I guess I should at least consider it, then," she conceded.

Gunderman shook his head. "No, no, no," he said. "Do you really think you can shoot a man dead, be caught literally holding the smoking gun, and get the same deal they give a teenager for hot-wiring a car? Don't be silly, Miss Carroll. It's 7 ½ to 15 *years*, and that's giving you a big break, partly because of your celebrity status, I imagine. It's certainly not the kind of deal they make with your average, everyday murderer. Fortunately for you, the State's Attorney is afraid that if he leans too hard on you, your fans will remember it at the ballot box, and he's up for re-election. Otherwise, the State wouldn't go any lower than Murder Two, with a minimum of 20 to 40…that's *years,* before you ask," he added ironically.

"Not interested," she said flatly, opening her hand, and allowing the paper to flutter to the floor. She crossed her arms over her chest and set her jaw defiantly. "I'd rather take my chances at trial, all or nothing."

He sighed. "It's a good thing I'm the lawyer and you're the client," he told her with exaggerated patience. "You *do* know that if you don't take the plea, you'll be tried for Murder One, don't you? And the sentence for that…, the *mandatory* sentence, meaning that the judge has no discretion in the matter…, makes 20 to 40 looks like after-school detention."

"Judicial enslavement, yes, I know." She scowled. "For Glawen's sake, Mr. Gunderman," she said, "that bastard was trying to *rape* me. I only did what I had to do to defend myself. The law says you're allowed to use deadly force to defend yourself from sexual assault. This is a clear case of self-defense, justifiable homicide, not murder, not a crime at all."

"Now look, Miss Carroll, reading a couple of law books in the prison library does not make you an attorney," Gunderman said, his patience beginning to fray. "We don't have any evidence of sexual assault. To begin with, there's no sign of a struggle."

"What about my torn blouse?" she demanded.

"You mean the torn blouse that your secretary didn't see when she came into your office and found you holding a smoking gun with Forsberg's corpse lying six feet away, on your couch?" Gunderman asked.

"Naturally, she wouldn't remember a little detail like a torn blouse, not when she saw a dead body right there in the room," she countered. "But the cops saw the torn blouse. It's in the report by that detective…whatsisname…"

"Olafur," Gunderman supplied the name. "Sure it is, because you pointed it out and told him it happened during the 'struggle.' But don't you think it will sound a little strange to the jury when they hear that you never screamed for help? To say nothing of the complete lack of bruises or marks on your body. Doesn't sound like much of a struggle, does it?"

"Don't worry you worry about *that*, Mr. Gunderman. I'll take care of that part. The jury will believe it, after I tell them how it happened," she said confidently. "By the time I'm done, everybody will feel so sorry for the poor, persecuted little schoolmarm, they'll be ready to ride the State's Attorney out of town on a rail."

Suddenly, she buried her face in her hands and wailed, "He said, 'I'm going to f-…fu-…I'm sorry, I can't repeat the word, but I'm certain you all know it. It is a crude term for sexual intercourse… and that he was going to have his way with me right then and there. Then he *attacked* me, leaped on me, like a savage beast! I fought him with all my might, but he was much stronger than me. When he tore my blouse, I knew that in a minute I would be stripped naked and thrown down across my desk, at his mercy!" She stopped to draw in a long, shuddering breath. "I suppose it must have been fear that gave me the strength to push him off. He fell to the floor." She sobbed and hid her face again. When she raised her head her tear-sodden features presented a distressing picture of innocence defiled. "Then he pulled a gun out from somewhere, from his jacket, I suppose, and snarled, 'I'll kill you!' Then he pointed his gun right at my head." She spoke with quiet intensity now, looking her attorney straight in the eye. "I caught his wrist, there was a struggle, and it…the gun…" she stopped and closed her eyes, as if the memory of that terrible moment was more than she could bear. Then she bravely went on, "…it went off. The next thing I knew…," one hand now crept to her mouth, "…he was lying on my sofa, all…all covered in bl-blood." She broke down, again burying her face in her hands. "He was dead,"

Then she looked up, perfectly composed, her voice cool, calm, and even. "Well, Mr. Gunderman," she asked, "*now* what do you think?"

He gazed at her with new respect. "You know, it might just work," he mused, half to himself. Then he said to Greta, "It would make my job a lot easier, though, if we could explain exactly why this Forsberg character was in your office in the first place. In her statement, your secretary Edda told the arresting officer ….," he dug into his briefcase and pulled out a manila folder, from which he extracted the sheets of flimsy blue paper of the police incident

39

report. He smoothed the papers out on the table and read, "'He said he was an old friend of Miss Carroll's, and he seemed like a nice enough sort, so I let him wait in her office until she returned from lunch.'" Gunderman looked at his client in inquiry. "So, how did you know him?"

"I didn't know him at all. He was a perfect stranger," she lied smoothly and without the slightest hesitation. "I never laid eyes on him in my life, before that day. Let the State prove otherwise. Can they?"

"No," Gunderman admitted, "at least, there's nothing about it in the discovery packet from the prosecutor. However, there are a couple of other bits of evidence we need to discuss before we decide if we should take this case to trial."

"Go ahead," she said immediately as if she was confident she knew the answers even before she heard his questions.

"Edda told the detectives that she remembered seeing a manila envelope and some photographs on your desk when she came into your office the first time," Gunderman said, looking at the police report again, "but, when she came back into your office, after calling the police from her phone, there was no sign of either the envelope or the pictures."

"Did Edda say she saw what or who was on these photographs?" Greta asked.

"No, she admitted she didn't get a good look at them," Gunderman said. "However, Detective Olafur found some scraps of heavy paper stock floating around in the toilet of your private bathroom which turned out to be pieces of torn-up photographs." He stopped and peered closely at his client. "I don't suppose you can tell me anything about where those scraps came from."

"You suppose correctly, counselor," Greta answered, smiling.

Gunderman stroked his chin thoughtfully. "It's an interesting case," he said. "While the State will have no problem proving that you were responsible for the decedent's death ...we aren't even contesting that ..., when it comes to motive, they've got nothing but a big hole. The State's Attorney has a dilemma: if you *didn't* kill him in self-defense, which you will claim, why *did* you do it? And without evidence of some other motive, that frightened schoolteacher routine of yours could be very persuasive, especially if we back it up with character witnesses, who will tell the jury what a wonderful, gentle, kindly...you-name-it...person you are. Yes," he said, nodding, "the more I consider it, the better I like your chances. Not that you have a sure thing," he added hastily. "There are no sure things, not in this business."

"I would have an even better chance if the jury heard what a dirtbag Forsberg was, wouldn't I?" Greta asked.

Gunderman looked at her sharply. "I thought you said he was a complete stranger and that you never laid eyes on him in your life, before that day in your office."

"Uh...yes, that's right," Greta said, momentarily flustered. She recovered quickly, and went on, "I simply assumed that any man who would attack a helpless woman as brazenly

41

as...what was his name again? Larson?... would have some sort of criminal record, that's all."

It was obvious from his expression that the skeptical Gunderman did not believe a word of this. "Miss Carroll, while I can't force you to trust me, you should understand that it's in your best interest to provide all the relevant information you have. If you are holding back some important fact, it will be impossible for me to accurately evaluate your case or properly prepare your defense. I remind you, your freedom is on the line here," he said sternly. "Now, is there *anything* you haven't told me that you think I should know? Anything that might possibly have a bearing on your case? Keep in mind that whatever you say will be kept in strict confidence, even if you admit to me that you committed the crime. It is protected by client-attorney privilege, which means that I am forbidden to repeat it to anyone else without your explicit permission. And even if I *did* commit a breach of ethics and reveal privileged information (and it hasn't happened yet, not in my 30 years as a member of the criminal bar), it *still* couldn't be used against you in court. So, if there is something about this case that you know and I don't, I strongly recommend that you tell what it is, *now*."

Greta made a great show of concentration, tilting her head back, frowning, and closing her eyes, as if diligently combing through her memory. "No, Mr. Gunderman," she said at last, "I can't think of a single thing."

42

Chapter Three: Trial by Jury

After the jury had been selected, and the twelve good men and true who would decide the fate of Miss Betty of the Wireless Schoolhouse were seated in the jury box, the court took a brief recess. The prosecutor, a sandy-haired, bespectacled lawyer named Ulf Stenstrom, waved Gunderman over to his table. He had the slightly absent-minded air of a professor, and appeared to be both young and harmless. Rolf Gunderman had tangled with Stenstrom before, and he knew the Assistant State's Attorney was about as harmless as one of his broadsword-wielding Viking ancestors.

"I want to offer your client one last chance to plead on this case," Stenstrom said. "I have nothing personal against Miss Betty…, in fact, I have 2 kids at home who listen to her show every day. I'm pretty sure they love her more than me. She's still a young woman, and I'd hate to see her throw away her whole life by trying to beat this case. 7 ½ to 15 isn't forever, and nobody will get too worked up about whether the decedent got justice. He was hardly a pillar of the community, after all."

"There's that," Rolf agreed, "plus the fact that your boss is up for re-election in six months, and he doesn't want to lose all those mommy votes, as the mean man who sent dear Miss Betty to the auction block."

Stenstrom shrugged. "That's as may be," he answered noncommittally. "But if she goes down on Murder One, it won't be the Big House for the

43

Wireless Schoolmarm; it'll be judicial enslavement..." he paused, then continued in a very serious tone, "...and she *is* going down, Rolf. I can promise you that."

Rolf Gunderman knew that Ulf Stenstrom was not inclined to bluff, and he also knew that the man was the State Attorney's lead homicide prosecutor for a good reason: he got convictions. As far as Rolf could tell, the state's case was far from air-tight, but Stenstrom's attitude suggested that there was more to it than met the eye. He wondered what the State had up its sleeve.

"I just can't see it, Ulf," he said. "You have a young, pretty, sympathetic woman who also happens to be a celebrity as your defendant, an unsympathetic corpse, no evidence connecting the two, no motive, and a reasonable self-defense claim. So what am I missing?"

Stenstrom did not answer directly. Instead, he asked, "Did you get the impression that your client is holding out on you? Based on what you're telling me, it's pretty obvious that she is, and the things you don't know about are going to come back to bite her on her pretty little ass." He glanced at Greta, who was just being brought out to the courtroom from her holding cell in the basement, then looked meaningfully back at Rolf. "Talk to her," he urged. "I'll leave the offer on the table until the judge gets back on the bench," he said. "But if she doesn't take it by then, her next stop will be the auction block. Because I have her, Rolf; I have her dead to rights," he finished with grim earnestness.

44

Gunderman was impressed. He did not know what made **the** prosecutor so confident, but he was convinced Stenstrom was telling him nothing less than the absolute, unadulterated truth. Unfortunately, while he could see it, he still couldn't get his client to agree. "You're telling me that my goose is cooked, that he has a hammer ready to mash me," Greta answered, badly mangling a metaphor. "Fine. I'll take the deal…" he started to congratulate her on her good sense, then stopped when she continued, "…just as soon as you tell me what has on me."

He shook his head. "I don't know, Miss Carroll," he admitted. "I can only advise you based on my thirty years of experience in criminal representation: whatever he has, I believe it's as good as says."

"Well, you can tell him thanks, but no thanks, Mr. Gunderman," she said. "I liked my chances yesterday, and nothing you said today has changed my mind. Now, are you ready to fight for me, or are you going to run up the white flag before we start? Tell me the truth: will I be better off if I fire you right now, and take over the defense myself?"

"A defendant who represents herself has a fool for a client and a shyster for a lawyer," he told her. He shook his head. "No, Miss Carroll, you would most definitely *not* be better off representing yourself. I will give this case all I've got, don't you worry about that. I haven't tanked one yet."

She nodded. "That's all I wanted to know." Rolf caught the eye of his opposite number, and shook his head, "No."

If Ulf Stenstrom was sitting on some massive bombshell, there was no sign of it during the State's direct case. The secretary, Edda Herold, was the first witness. She testified that she heard loud bangs coming from Miss Betty's office, and had entered whereupon she saw her boss standing behind her desk holding a pistol, and a bloody corpse draped awkwardly over the sofa a few feet away.

"Did you notice anything unusual about Miss Carroll's clothing at that time?" Stenstrom asked.

"Objection," Rolf said, popping up. "Leading."

"Sustained," the judge responded. "Could you rephrase that question, Mr. Stenstrom?"

The Assistant State's Attorney rolled his eyes heavenward. "What, if anything, did you notice that was unusual about Miss Carroll when you entered her office?" He asked.

"Other than the fact that she was holding a gun, do you mean?" the witness answered. She hesitated. "I didn't notice anything special …but I was so shocked when I saw that man… Mr. Forsberg, that was his name, wasn't it…? When I saw him lying there, all bloody, I didn't take time out to look Miss Carroll over."

"Did Miss Carroll say anything when you came in?" Stenstrom asked.

"Yes," Edda answered, this time without hesitation. "She said...screamed, really… 'Edda, go call an ambulance, call the police! Hurry!' So, I went right back out to my desk, called emergency, and told the dispatcher what happened."

46

"Now what, if anything, out of the ordinary did you see in Miss Carroll's office when you entered?" The prosecutor asked.

"Objection," Rolf said, getting back up. "Leading."

The judge shook his head. "Overruled." To the witness, he said, "You may answer."

Edda closed her eyes as if she was trying to bring back the image. "There was a manila envelope, lying open on her desk," she said slowly, "and what looked like photographs had fallen out and were spread over the desk."

"Your witness," Stenstrom said.

Rolf followed up on the prosecutor's last question immediately. "You didn't see what was depicted on those photographs, did you, Miss Herold?" He asked, expecting her to admit she hadn't.

He was surprised when she answered, "I *think* the one on top of the pile might have been a picture of two people in a bed, but I can't be sure."

He tried to mend whatever damage her answer had caused. "But you only had a very brief glance at it, correct?"

"That's true, Mr. Gunderman," Edda agreed.

"In fact, as you sit here today, you cannot say with any degree of certainty who or what was in that photograph, can you?" He persisted.

She considered, then said, "No, sir, I can't."

Encouraged, he went on. "In fact, it is entirely possible that whatever you saw on Miss Carrol's desk in that brief moment might not have been photographs at all, isn't that right?"

Edda frowned. "When you put it that way, Mr. Gunderman, I suppose that's so," she answered. "I could have been mistaken about seeing photographs."

Gunderman could now feel the wind at his back. He asked, "And when you returned after calling for help, a very a short time later, there was neither an envelope nor any photographs on Miss Carroll's desk, was there?"

She nodded. "That is correct."

The witness had become so cooperative that he decided to take a chance. "So, isn't it possible that you might have been mistaken about seeing the envelope and photographs that you previously testified?" Normally, Rolf would not have asked a prosecution witness such a question, but he sensed that Edda was a reluctant witness for the State, who probably was fond of Miss Betty and wanted to help her. The risk was not very great: at worst, her answer would simply confirm the existence of the pictures, which Stenstrom could not produce or connect to anything.

As it turned out, he had nothing to worry about. The witness came through with the answer he wanted. "That's true, Mr. Gunderman," she said. "There may not have been any pictures at all: I could have been mistaken about that." She turned to face the jury. "I was only there for a few seconds, and I was frightened nearly out of my wits at the time. I remember that when I saw the man lying there, I became so dizzy, I very nearly fainted; that's how upset I was. So, Mr. Gunderman, if you want the absolute truth..." she paused.

48

"Oh yes, Miss Herold," Gunderman said earnestly, "not only do *I* want the absolute truth, but so does the judge, the jury, and my colleague, Mr. Stenstrom. You may take my word for it."

Edda again addressed her remarks directly to the jury. "Well, the truth is," she said, "as I think back on it, I was so confused and frightened that I can't be sure I correctly remember anything I saw or heard that day."

Gunderman resisted an urge to pinch himself to make sure he wasn't dreaming. Had he actually just heard the State's own witness torpedo their case? It was almost unbelievable. He was so bemused, the judge had to remind him that he was still in the middle of his cross-examination.

"Do you have any more questions for this witness, Mr. Gunderman?" the be-wigged jurist prompted.

"Ah, uh …yes, just one or two, thank you, Your Lordship," he answered. He recalled that he and the client had decided to ask the State's principal witness to testify as to the former's good character. This was somewhat unusual, to be sure, but far from unheard-of. Certainly, if there had been any doubt about where Edda Herald's loyalties lay, they had been put to rest by her testimony on cross-examination. "Your Lordship, in the interest of efficiency, I ask the Court's permission to elicit character evidence from this witness at this time, rather than inconveniencing her by making her return to testify during the defense case," he said.

"Do you have any objection, Mr. Stenstrom?" the judge asked.

"No, Your Lordship," the Assistant States Attorney answered. "I can think of no reason why this witness should be inconvenienced."

He's certainly being a good sport about it, Gunderman thought, *especially considering the way she just punched a big hole below the waterline in his case. If she had done that to me, I don't think I would mind inconveniencing her a little bit.*

"Then you may proceed, Mr. Gunderman," the judge said.

With a few questions, Gunderman elicited the fact that Edda Herold had been Miss Betty's secretary for 5 years. She then was obliged to modify her answer, by identifying her employer as the defendant, Elizabeth Carroll. Edda further stated that she was familiar with Miss Betty's...that is, Miss *Carroll's* reputation in the community, and concluded that said reputation for peacefulness and truthfulness, as well as for being law-abiding, were all of the very highest order. She added that Miss Carroll was the most wonderful person she, Edda Herold, had ever known. Rolf Gunderman expected to hear this additional paean to his client's saintliness be stricken from the record after an objection from Stenstrom, since it was Edda's personal opinion, and therefore inadmissible. [Note: Both here and in the WP, character testimony is limited by the Rules of Evidence to a defendant's *reputation* in the community. The witness may not offer the jury his or her personal opinion of the defendant, strange though it may seem, as this is considered too unreliable to meet the minimum standard for relevance. CJB.] The usually razor-

50

sharp Stenstrom must have been asleep at the switch, because he did not object.

The rest of the State's case did not take very long to present. Dr. Bergmann, the coroner, made a brief appearance to tell the jury what everyone already knew: that the decedent had died from the wounds caused by multiple gunshots to his chest. There was some equally abbreviated testimony from the arresting officer, who testified about the defendant's torn clothing, but also noted the absence of any injuries indicative of a struggle. Finally, Detective Olafur, the assigned investigator, described the recovery of a half-dozen scraps of paper from the commode in the defendant's private bathroom. Rather than require the prosecution to call their forensic expert, Gunderman stipulated to the police laboratory's report, which concluded that the scraps were pieces of one or more photographs, and allowed the detective to read the report from the stand. The evidence was harmless, as far as he could tell, since there was no evidence of what was in the pictures and the State could not connect them to any other evidence. Olafur also showed the eight-chambered .27 caliber revolver to the jury, which the defense conceded was the fatal weapon.

Gunderman held his breath when the detective left the stand. If Stenstrom had a blockbuster witness in his back pocket, this would be the time to call him. He let out a gusty sigh of relief when the Assistant State's Attorney spoke the words he was hoping to hear: "The State rests." The judge immediately banged down his gavel and adjourned the case, telling the jury to be back in the box by 9 AM sharp.

Client and defense counsel were apparently thinking along the same lines. Before Gunderman could say anything, Greta asked. "That's *it*? That's their whole case? What happened to their big secret weapon?" She demanded. When he shrugged in reply, she continued, "How does that great plea offer look *now*, Mr. 30-Years-in-the-Business?"

"It looks like you were right and I was wrong, Miss Carroll," he conceded. "But the case is not over yet, not by a long shot. You still have to sell your self-defense story to the jury, and make it hold up under cross-examination."

She rose when two guards appeared to escort her back to her cell. "Hi, boys," she said. She stood up, then wagged a finger at Rolf Gunderman. "Don't try to teach your grandma to suck eggs...*echh*! Where did *that* disgusting expression come from? Don't worry about *me*, Mr. Gunderman. You concentrate on the legal mumbo-jumbo, and I'll take care of the jury."

"Yes sir, ma'am," he answered, giving her a mock salute, before the guards led her away.

Chapter Four: Rules of Evidence

When the defense case opened the next morning, Greta was the first witness. She seemed both guileless and defenseless, as she recalled her narrow escape from a fate worse than death, and convincingly enacted the part of an honest witness who was innocent of all wrongdoing. Moreover, she accomplished this while simultaneously making Rolf and every other man in the courtroom aware of the fact that she was one of the most beautiful women any of them had ever seen. *No, not* beautiful. he corrected himself mentally. *Beautiful is not the right word. It would be more accurate to say that she was the most* desirable *female he had ever laid eyes on.*

While on the surface Greta was the picture of a virginal, young schoolteacher who took ten showers a day, whose thoughts were as clean as her untouched body, somehow, without doing anything one could point to, she gave the impression that her pure-as-driven-snow exterior was only a façade covering a simmering volcano of sexuality. Gunderman, the jurors, the court officers, male spectators, even the judge, hung on her every word and movement. When she casually uncrossed, then re-crossed her long legs, Rolf imagined he heard popping noises made by male eyeballs exploding out of their sockets.

He was a little surprised by Ulf Stenstrom's nonchalant cross-examination; after all, the case would turn on whether the jury believed this witness, and Rolf was aware of certain weak points in her story that the prosecutor could exploit. But Stenstrom only made what Rolf considered a perfunctory attempt to poke holes in the defense. He contented himself with asking Greta to confirm her testimony that she had no personal quarrel with Lars Forsberg, had not known him, and furthermore, had never, to her knowledge, so much as seen the man in her entire life him, before the day of the shooting.

After offering a half-dozen character witnesses, all of whom eagerly to told the jury that the defendant had a sterling reputation for truthfulness, honesty, and was renowned throughout the community for her law-abidingness (Rolf thought this last was unlikely; he sincerely doubted that the community had ever discussed whether Miss Betty was law-abiding,) and the defense rested.

"Does the State have anything else to present before closing arguments?" the judge asked Stenstrom.

"Thank you, Your Lordship," the prosecutor answered, rising. "As a matter of fact, the State intends to present an extensive rebuttal case. May we approach?" He walked around his table, and up to the judge's bench, motioning for Rolf to join him. "I suspect that Mr. Gunderman will wish to make argument on the admissibility of some or all of my rebuttal evidence, so I suggest that Your Lordship recess the case, so we can discuss it out of the presence of the jury."

The judge looked at Gunderman, who nodded, then said, "The jury will take a luncheon recess. Please return by 2 o'clock." He banged down his gavel and rose to his feet. "I will see you both in my chambers in ten minutes."

Rolf returned to the defense table, where Greta awaited him. For the first time, she showed a crack in her armor of self-confidence.

"What were you talking about up there?" she demanded. "What's going on?"

"You remember that hammer we decided Stenstrom didn't have?" he asked. She nodded.

"Well, I think you are about to find out the same thing the frost giants did when Thor bashed their brains out with Mjolnir," he answered. "I suspect that the Assistant State's Attorney is about to wield his hammer...and I predict it will be a great, big one."

He turned and followed Ulf Stenstrom back to the judge's chambers.

***

The two attorneys sat facing the judge who looked back from behind his imposingly huge desk. "Well, Mr. Stenstrom," the judge asked, "what sport of surprise evidence do you have for us, and why did you not present whatever it is during your direct case?"

"We have several items, Your Lordship," the prosecutor responded, "all of which I believe are appropriately presented in rebuttal. First, I will call a Mr. Helmut Carlson, who owns a pawnshop on Westbridge Street here in New Stavanger. He will testify that he sold the murder weapon to the defendant. This is being introduced to impeach the defendant's testimony that the gun was the decedent's, not hers. It would not have been relevant on direct."

"Well, Mr. Gunderman," the judge asked, "can you give me any reason why I should exclude Mr. Carlson's testimony?" Although Rolf thought there was a pretty good case for bringing it in on direct as evidence of his client's intent, he knew he would not win on that point. "No, Your Lordship," he answered reluctantly.

"What else do you have up your sleeve, Mr. Stenstrom?" the judge asked.

"I have a certified record showing that the defendant now known as Elizabeth Carroll was born as Greta Lundgren, and had her name changed by petition in West Faroes County," he said. "We couldn't possibly have introduced it in the case-in-chief, Your Lordship, or Mr. Gunderman would have, quite properly, objected to it as inadmissible character evidence," he continued blandly, studying his opponent for his reaction. "Why, the jury might think the defendant was trying to hide something, and that would hardly be fair to her, would it?"

"I deeply appreciate the State's concern for my client," Rolf said ironically, "but I didn't happen to see the name change evidence in the discovery packet, and since you failed to provide it, I would ask the court to exclude it, under Rule 4.6 of the Rules of Criminal Procedure: failure to provide mandatory pre-trial discovery to opposing counsel."

"I am afraid I will have to rule against you, Mr. Gunderman," the judge said. "There are exceptions to the mandatory discovery rule that may have slipped your mind, one of which is directly on point here. Rule 11 of the Rules of Evidence, specifically names rebuttal evidence as one of those exceptions."

Of course it hadn't slipped his mind: Rolf Gunderman knew the Rules of Evidence backward and forward. He simply wanted to show Stenstrom and the judge that he wasn't giving up without a fight. Not that it made any difference, he admitted. He nodded, and said, "Yes, Your Lordship."

"Finally," Stenstrom continued, "I will call a Mr. Arthur Pellinger, Public Witness." He handed a packet of stapled papers to Rolf and another to the judge. "This is Mr. Pellinger's statement, which he made to a detective in my office three days after the death of Mr. Forsberg. I believe it speaks for itself."

Rolf Gunderman did not need to read very far into Pellinger's statement before he knew that he was looking at the State's secret weapon. He did not have to read much further than that, before he knew that, as Stenstrom had predicted, his client was on a one-way trip to the auction block.

***

"Mr. Pellinger," Stenstrom asked, "could you please tell the jury when, where, and under what circumstances you first met the decedent, Mr. Forsberg?"

Arthur Pellinger was a tall man with a thin face. He had a precise, fussy manner that the horn-rimmed reading glasses he lowered onto his nose emphasized. He looked down at the open appointment resting on the rail of the witness stand, cleared his throat, and said, "Mr. Forsberg entered my office for a consultation at approximately 12:33

in the afternoon, of Freysday, September 13 of this year. That was three days before his death. It was the first and only time I met him."

"Can you tell the jury the reason for his visit?" The State's Attorney asked.

"Objection," Gunderman barked, jumping up. "Calls for a hearsay response." He knew he could not stop this evidence from coming in, but he hoped to at least disrupt the process a little.

"Overruled," the judge said. He addressed the jury. "As I have explained to you previously, normally a witness may not testify about what someone else has said to him. That is called hearsay, and it is *usually* inadmissible, but not always. This is one of the exceptions to that rule. Mr. Pellinger has been qualified as a licensed Public Witness, whose profession involves preserving information for clients, and when he is testifying in his professional capacity, the hearsay rule does not apply." He turned back to the witness. "You may answer."

***

"First of all," Lars Forsberg said, "I need a promise from you that whatever I tell you will not be repeated...to anybody."

"You have nothing to fear on that score, Mr. Forsberg," Pellinger assured him. "When you consult me in my capacity as a licensed Public Witness, I am required by law to keep whatever you tell me is confidential, and no one, not even the National Police Bureau, can force me to reveal a single word of it."

The furtive little man nodded. "That's what I thought. So, let me be frank with you. I was recently released from prison, and I'm trying to get my life started up again, you know?"

Pellinger nodded. He *did* know. After many years as a Witness and long experience with the type, he had identified Forsberg as a jailbird the moment he came through the door.

"Well, I'm going to see an old friend, to ask her for a job with her company," Forsberg continued. "But we haven't been in touch for a while, so I'm a *little* worried that she might not want to associate with me anymore, being that I'm an ex-con and all..." he paused. Pellinger waited. He had a fairly good idea of what was coming next.

"Well, I kept some...um...souvenirs from the old days, to remind her of how much we meant to each other back then, just in case she forgets. You can't assume old friends will always remember these kinds of things, if you know what I mean."

Pellinger nodded again. "Indeed," he said, noncommittally.

Forsberg opened his shabby leather briefcase and drew out a fat manila envelope, which he handed to the Public Witness. "Her real name is Greta Lundgren, but nowadays she calls herself Betty Carroll. She's better known as Miss Betty of the Wireless Schoolhouse." Pellinger, who was in the act of removing the contents of the envelope, stopped, looked at his new client with raised eyebrows, and asked, "Is that so?"

"It certainly is," Forsberg agreed. "To be honest..." [Pellinger wondered idly when the last time the word could be applied to Forsberg] "…I'm not sure what kind of welcome home I'll get, so I wanted a little…insurance, let's just say, in case Greta doesn't react well when I show up on her doorstep. Not that she would do anything violent, but you never know about people."

Pellinger paged quickly through the material Forsberg had given him, to get a general idea of the contents. It consisted of photographs, newspaper articles, and court records relating to Greta Lundgren's role in a series of blackmail schemes that had resulted in Forsberg's conviction and imprisonment

The articles and records established that the 17-year-old Betty Carroll, or Greta Lundgren, as she was then known, had been Forsberg's partner in a criminal enterprise, the extortion of money from male victims, operating what is known in the underworld as a "badger game." Photographs from the envelope showed the partially-clothed defendant in compromising positions with various men. These were what Forsberg used to squeeze the johns who balked at paying up. Forsberg instructed Pellinger to take the contents to the appropriate authority in the event something sudden and permanent happened to him after his meeting with Betty Carroll.

By the time Arthur Pellinger left the witness stand, the jury, who had practically fallen in love with Miss Betty during her testimony, were now looking at her as if she was something that had just crawled out from under a rock.

The court took another recess before closing arguments. Greta no longer seemed so confident. "It doesn't look very good for our side, does it, Mr. Gunderman?" She asked.

He tried to think of a way to sugar-coat his answer and failed. "No," he answered flatly, "it does not."

"I don't understand one thing," she said. "Why didn't Stenstrom introduce all his evidence right away, instead of waiting until after all our witnesses had testified?"

"Because he is a smart lawyer, damn it," Rolf answered. "A lot of his rebuttal evidence might have been kept out by the judge on direct, as inadmissible character evidence. But after we put all those character witnesses on the stand, who told the jury what a wonderful reputation you have for truthfulness, honesty, and law-abidingness, we opened the door for him to rebut them with evidence that you are in reality a liar and a criminal."

"That's not fair!" she protested. "All those things I did with Lars happened such a long time ago. Anyway, I was just a kid back then."

He did not respond to this irrelevancy. "Probably the most damaging testimony was when you told the jury that Forsberg had tried to rape you. When you said that, you opened the door for Stenstrom to impeach you with Pellinger's evidence, which showed that Forsberg was blackmailing you, which gave you an excellent motive to murder him. If you hadn't testified at all, I might have been able to keep that blackmail evidence out of the record altogether."

He paused and shook his head. "You should have come clean with me, Miss Lundgren," he said sadly. "If you had told me the truth..." he trailed off. What was the point, now?

Rolf gave the best closing argument he could, although in his heart, he knew it could only end one way. "Members of the jury, it is true that my client was not wholly candid with you when she testified," he admitted. "But consider what would have happened to her reputation, if the evidence of some bad decisions she made as a teenager..., remember, she was only 17 years old when she and Forsberg were arrested..., had become public knowledge, and she was trying to prevent that. Betty Carroll is a celebrity, idolized by millions of little children, and Forsberg's revelations would have destroyed her career, as in fact they doubtless already have. If you find her guilty, then you are ensuring that the blackmailer, Lars Forsberg, wins after all. I would ask you to consider one more thing: is the world a worse place or a better one, now that it no longer contains a man named Lars Forsberg? Does Betty Carroll truly deserve to be reduced to a chattel slave for ridding society of this persistent, unrepentant malefactor, a man who set to work devising new criminal schemes from almost the day he finished serving time for his old ones? Or she should instead be commended for the performance of an unpleasant but necessary task, one that our legal system was unwilling or unable to do."

His arguments had a certain surface appeal, he thought, and they might have momentarily swayed a few of the jurors. But Ulf Stenstrom's closing statement mercilessly exposed the basically shoddy nature of Rolf's arguments.

"Does Betty Carroll deserve praise, rather than punishment for her deeds, as Mr. Gunderman would have it?" Stenstrom demanded. "Should we give her a good conduct ribbon for murdering a man in cold blood, award her the key to the city for taking the life of another human being, all for the noble goal of keeping her criminal past a secret? Here in Sylvania, we have abolished capital punishment, because we believe that no one, not even the State is wise enough to make the ultimate decision of who may live and who must die. Indeed, if, as I expect, you find the defendant guilty at the end of this trial, she will be a direct beneficiary of that enlightened policy, for she will not be hanged, as in former times, but rather judicially enslaved. Shall we instead invest a Betty Carroll with that godlike power, appoint her as the arbiter of life and death? Because, if you find her not guilty, as Mr. Gunderman urges, that is exactly what you will be doing...

"Mr. Gunderman tells us that she acted for the benefit of the community. Rubbish! If she had given a pin for the community, she would have called the police and had Forsberg arrested for extortion. That is what a decent citizen..., no, that is what a decent *human being* would have done, for the good of society. But the good of society was the last thing Betty Carroll was thinking about. By her actions, she has demonstrated that she puts herself and her personal interests first, last, and always, ahead of everything and everyone, while the welfare of society never enters the equation. She decided that murder would best serve her selfish purposes, and she acted accordingly. Did she at least show remorse for her crime, indicate that she had some recognition of the seriousness of what she had done in taking the life of another human being? No. Instead of accepting responsibility for murdering her old friend, Lars Forsberg, she tried to evade it with fabrication, by lying, first to the police, then to you jurors, here in court. She looked you right in the eye, one by one, and made a show of being a frightened innocent, to win your sympathy. But bit was all a sham, a trick. The woman now known as Betty Carroll lied to you, members of the jury, lied brazenly, lied through her teeth, lied systematically, lied without the slightest qualm, right after taking an oath to tell the truth....

"There can be no question of Betty Carroll's intent in this case, gentlemen of the jury. It could not be made any plainer after you consider a single piece of evidence: the number of times she shot Lars Forsberg. If she had pulled the trigger just once, perhaps, *perhaps* we could have generously concluded that the shooting was a sudden, thoughtless act, a reaction to a highly stressful situation and that she really had not meant to kill Forsberg. If that had been the case, she might have been guilty of the lesser crime of manslaughter, but not of murder. But when the evidence showed that she fired her weapon eight times, pumped not one but *eight* steel-jacketed slugs in Lars Forsberg's body, there is only one reasonable conclusion you can reach: that the defendant took the life of Lars

Forsberg intentionally, purposefully, and with malice aforethought, that in short, that she committed the crime of murder in the first degree, and nothing less. Gentlemen of the jury, Betty Carroll is a liar and a murderess, and after you have considered all the evidence in this case, I ask that you remain true to the oath each of you swore at the start of this trial, and find the defendant guilty of Murder in the First Degree."

At the judge's suggestion, they waited in the courtroom for a while after the jury went out to deliberate so that they would not have to recall all the parties, if the jury was able to come to a verdict within a couple of hours, which in Rolf Gunderman's opinion, was likely. "I guess I shouldn't have testified, after all," Greta told him. "If had just kept my mouth shut, I might have had a chance to beat this thing."

He shook his head. "I don't think so," he answered. "Without your testimony, all the jury would have heard was uncontradicted evidence that you shot Forsberg multiple times with your own gun. Even without any blackmail evidence, that's an easy win for the State. If you don't take the stand and raise a defense of some kind, the jury is not going to conjure one up to rescue you, Miss Carroll."

As Rolf expected, it did not take very long for the jury to reach a verdict. Less than an hour after they went out to deliberate, they were back in the jury box, and the foreman was handing the court clerk the verdict sheet. The judge took the verdict sheet from the clerk, looked it over, and nodded

65

once. The Cryer announced, "The defendant will rise." Greta stood and faced the judge with Rolf Gunderman at her side.

"Betty Carroll, the jury has found you guilty of Murder in the First Degree," the judge intoned. He looked at the jurors. "So say you all?" He asked. Each of the 12 men nodded or said, "Yes." The judge continued, "The jury is dismissed with thanks for your service."

The judge turned back to address the attorneys. "Since there is a mandatory penalty for this offense, unless one of the parties objects, I will waive the standard pre-trial investigation and report, and proceed to sentencing immediately. Does either counsel object, or have anything they feel should be brought to the court's attention at this time?"

"No, Your Lordship," Stenstrom answered.

"Since, as the Court has stated, there is absolutely no discretion in the imposition of the sentence," Rolf said, "I see no point in wasting Your Lordship's time or my breath."

"Does the defendant wish to address the Court before sentence is imposed?" the judge asked Greta.

"Yes, Your Lordship," she said. "I don't suppose anybody will believe me now, but for whatever it's worth, the truth is that Lars really *did* try to rape me in my office. That's all I wanted to say."

The judge's expression suggested that he did not believe it was worth very much at all. "Elizabeth Carroll, you have been found guilty of Murder in the First Degree. Therefore, I will now

66

impose the prescribed penalty of judicial enslavement. You are hereby stripped of all rights as a citizen, and as of this moment and henceforward, you are a chattel slave. Furthermore, it is ordered that you shall remain permanently in that condition and you may not be freed or manumitted during the remainder of your natural existence. Pursuant to Section 2501 of the Criminal Code, relating to forfeitures, you shall be sold at a time and place designated by the Sheriff of this County, with the proceeds of said sale going to the State Victim's Compensation Fund. So ordered and decreed." He banged down his gavel, then said, "Let the verdict be recorded," rose, gathered his robes about himself, and left the bench.

Greta, stunned by the suddenness of her enslavement, sat as if paralyzed. When the guards came to lead her away, she looked like a wind-up toy whose spring has run down.

Chapter Five: Research

A slightly built young woman, clad only in tortoise shell spectacles and a nervous expression, tip-toed quietly into the walnut-paneled library, timidly approaching the man seated in a large, upholstered armchair. There was nothing obviously intimidating about the man's appearance to justify the be-spectacled woman's obvious apprehension. He was a rather mild-looking fellow, neatly dressed in a tweed suit, in his late 50's or early 60's, with a slight paunch, with black hair turning to gray around his ears. His features were settled in a mildly contemplative expression and he could have easily been mistaken by someone who didn't know him for academic, a professor of history, or perhaps theology.

In fact, the man was no more a professor than he was mild. His name was Rupert Caine, and he was, among other things, the owner of the naked young woman, Dane Edberg, by name. Dane had excellent reasons for being nervous in Caine's presence, because he was an unusually harsh, demanding master, who did not hesitate to administer cruel and ingenious punishments at the drop of a hat, or sometimes, even before a hat had been dropped.

In the unlikely event that Dane had forgotten what happened to a slave who displeased Caine, he had provided a visual reminder on this occasion. Strapped in a frame of gleaming metal rods beside his chair, bent agonizingly backward and immovably bound, was another naked slave, a magnificently built woman with a thick mane of red-gold hair. Her arms had been bound together behind her back at the elbows, and her wrists were cuffed to the base of the frame near the floor. Her neck was confined in a metal collar at the end of a short rod projecting from the frame. The collar was adjusted so that the unfortunate woman's head was held inverted an inch or two above the floor, so that she looked at Caine upside-down and backward. A horizontal steel bar pressed into her spine just above the waist, to ensure that her back remained in an impossibly tight, elegant arc.

This combination of restraints forced the redhead to arch her superb form up in a startling and provocative display. Her full breasts thrust out from her chest as if they were begging to be handled, while her thighs were spread wide apart and her hips were raised invitingly. There was an oversized ring-gag stuffed into her mouth behind her teeth, allowing an uncontained river of drool to issue from her gaping lips and run down her cheeks in streams. Her tongue extended a remarkably long way out from the ring to wash the hirsute, wrinkled sack of Caine's testicles with single-minded intensity. The only interruption to this intimate service occurred from time to time when she would stop licking to howl briefly in agony after Caine lightly flicked her breasts or sex lips with the short silvery rod he held in one hand. But as soon as she regained control of her tongue again, she instantly resumed cleansing his sex.

Dane was familiar with both the woman and the device being used to punish her. Her name was Ulrika Torvald. She was the former Governor of Karlsvania, who had been impeached, convicted, removed from office, and sentenced to judicial enslaved after being convicted of crimes ranging from conspiracy to commit murder to abuse of public office. Ulrika had at one time been Dane's boss, and she had persuaded the younger woman to falsely confess to Ulrika's crimes in a desperate effort to escape justice. While in the end, the scheme had not saved Ulrika, it had resulted in Dane's enslavement for crimes she had never committed. It is therefore easy to understand why Dane, who had at one time had practically worshipped Ulrika, now hated her more than she did anything or anyone else in the universe. [More about Dane, Ulrika, their crimes and punishment, and many other things can be found in *By Judicial Decree 8: High Crimes and Misdemeanors*. CJB]

Despite her amply justified antipathy for the fallen governor, Dane could not help shuddering in sympathy each time the innocent-looking silver rod made contact with Ulrika's flesh, causing her to hurl herself madly against the metal bars and straps that held her, and scream until the veins stood out on her forehead. The skinny rod was a Neuro-Corrector, a slave-training device that employed direct stimulation of the pain receptors in the nervous system to induce extremely high levels of pain without inflicting any corresponding physical damage. It was this latter characteristic that made the Neuro-Corrector and Caine's other DNS (Direct

Nerve Stimulation) gadgets his favorite instruments for punishing his slaves. Since these devices did not cause physical injury, the only real limit to their use was the tendency of certain of his slave-girls to fall unconscious after only a few strokes. Ulrika, to her misfortune, stood up to the shocks rather well, and contrary to her desires and heartfelt prayers, did not faint, even after extended sessions under the Neuro-Corrector. Dane recalled her sole encounter with the device, and winced.

Although her bare feet made no sound on the thick Oriental carpet and his back was to the library door, Caine somehow was immediately aware of Dane's presence as soon as she entered the room. Without turning around to see who, if anyone was there, he asked, "Did you have any difficulty finding the information I wanted, Dane?"

By the way he phrased this question, it was evident that Caine assumed that she had succeeded. The very fact that she had returned at all was good evidence that she had accomplished the mission; Dane would not have dared to return to tell him that she had failed. Had she done so, she would have probably ended up like Ulrika, on the other side of his chair, being corrected with strokes of the little silver rod.

Dane rushed to his side, with the magazine she carried thrust out before her. "It was no trouble at all, Mr. Caine, sir," she answered. "*Notable Trials*..." (this was a monthly national journal that covered important legal cases) "... published the complete trial transcript."

Caine opened the magazine read for a time without speaking, then nodded. " Thank you, Dane," he said, pretending not to notice her sigh of relief. "Could you kindly give Master Quentin my compliments, and ask him to join me here at his earliest convenience?"

"Yes, Master, right away," Dane answered, and rushed out of the library. Caine picked up a telephone, spoke briefly, then sat back down in his chair. "Good news for you, my dear," he told the earnestly licking former governor. "In just a few days, I am going to be far too busy with a new slave to have the time to attend to you. Perhaps a quick going-away fuck would be in order before I send you back down to your cell. What do you think?"

"Uh-ehh uhhh ohh ayyy, ahhh-ah," she responded, this being the closest approximation the ring-gag permitted to, "Whatever you say, Master."

Caine turned his chair in a quarter-circle, until he was directly behind her, then stood up between her open thighs. He unzipped his trousers and presented his stiff rod to Ulrika's denuded pubic mound (Caine wanted his women hairless below the neck, and consequently, like his other fuck-toys, Ulrika's cleft was a bald as an egg.)

Caine patted the pockets of his jacket, then delved inside one and came out with a tube of ointment. As he unscrewed the cap and squeezed some of the translucent salve over his fingertips, he remarked, "It's been a while for you, hasn't it, Ulrika?" He gently rubbed some of the substance into the lips of her sex, taking special care to roll the bud of her clitoris carefully in his fingers, until it

72

was well coated with the greasy gel and stiff with excitement.

The tube contained one of Caine's most potent training instruments: a powerful aphrodisiac, which had a dramatic effect on female genitalia. Almost before he had released Ulrika's love button, her hips were weaving in an obscene dance, and she was breathing heavily. Caine nodded appreciatively at the sight, then applied the cream to other strategic portions of her anatomy.

"So, I thought that since I have neglected your sexual needs for so long," Caine continued, coming around to one side to capture her nipples, work the aphrodisiac into them, then tease, tug and pinch the little brown buttons until they stood at stiffly at attention, "I should make the experience memorable."

It was true that he had only rarely chosen Ulrika as his sexual partner since he had broken her to his will and trained her to serve him. An important element of Caine's training was the instilling of a powerful desire for intercourse, and after that training was complete, his slaves found that on the one hand, nothing excited them quite as much as bondage and flagellation followed by copulation, but on the other, without these preliminaries, they were quite unable to achieve orgasms. While Ulrika truly was suffering terrible, almost unbearable agony under Caine's rod, at the same time, her conditioning caused the harsh punishment and painful restraints to arouse her to an uncontrollable peak of sexual excitement. The deft strokes of Caine's fingers on her artificially stimulated nipples and clit brought her to the edge of a huge orgasm in practically no time.

"Eee ahh-eh, *eee!*" She begged, her tone and the extravagant movements of her pelvis making plain to him that she was attempting to say, "Please Master, *please!*"

Caine shook his head. "Now, you've been here long enough to know the rules, Ulrika," he admonished, taking his hand out of her dripping slot. She groaned and futilely thrust her hips in his general direction. "You will come when I give you permission, and not before. Remember?"

She nodded, then stared up at him, her eyes wild with need. She remembered all right: it would have been impossible to forget all those nights in Caine's dungeon, being conditioned to respond to both strokes of his hands and strokes of his whips, until he could control her body with either pleasure, pain, or a combination of the two, and now, she had no say in the matter.

Caine squatted down, reached into her open mouth, and after a short struggle, dislodged the metal ring holding her jaws apart. "Hak oo asser," Ulrika said, her speech of thanks blurred by her inability to control her exhausted jaw muscles.

"Not at all, my dear," Caine said genially. "It would be impossible for you to speak coherently with that ring in there, and as you know, I consider the verbal aspects of sex as important as the physical ones." She nodded.

"So why don't you start by begging to swallow my cock?" he asked. He rubbed his turgid organ lightly over her face by way of encouragement.

Speaking slowly and pronouncing each word carefully, Ulrika said, "Please Master Caine, will you kindly permit this slave to suck your great manhood?"

"Would you like that, Ulrika?" Caine inquired. "Would that be exciting for you?"

The former politician, who had at one time boasted that there was no-one in the world that she could not con, looked up from her knees at Caine, her blue eyes wide and utterly empty of guile, and said softly, "More than anything in the world, Master," and there was no doubt in his mind that she meant every word. Caine had crushed her so thoroughly that she no longer considered attempting to deceive him about even the smallest thing.

Caine considered the magnificent woman kneeling at his feet for a little while, enjoying the way her body trembled with a mixture of pent-up desire and fear that he might deny her. "Oh, all right," he said, with every appearance of reluctance, "if it's that important to you."

When Ulrika beamed in delight and leaned closer to envelop the head of his cock, Caine ordered "Get your ass up high and spread those knees. I'm going to stimulate you with this crop." He displayed an eighteen-inch long metal rod wrapped in braided strips of brown leather.

Ulrika rolled her eyes up at the crop momentarily, then assumed the position demanded by Caine, arching her back and moving her knees well apart as she slowly, expertly swallowed his shaft. She rolled her eyes nervously when she felt the cool, polished leather saw up and down on the lips of her sex and the tiny starburst of her anus, but she did not cease pleasuring Caine with her mouth for an instant.

Caine drew up the crop, examined it, then shook his head and clucked his tongue. He leaned forward and held the crop right before her eyes. "Look at that," he ordered. "It's covered with your pussy juice. Were you always such a shameless slut, Ulrika?" He put one hand on the back of her head, and forced his cock in deeper, until he could see how deeply he was buried from the visible bulge in her throat.

"Don't stop!" He snapped, then began to beat her rectum and pussy with vicious blows of the crop. Ulrika made muffled squeals of agony, which Caine experienced as delightful vibrations on the head of his cock. She was unable to completely control the actions of her lower body, which weaved madly from side to side as an involuntary reaction to the explosions of pain, but she neither attempted to dodge the crop or protect herself in any way, nor did she cease to wash his cock in her mouth, even as she approached unconsciousness from lack of oxygen.

"You like that, do you, cunt?" Caine growled. He pulled out just before he came, then held his spurting cock in his hand, to direct long, gleaming threads of his seed onto Ulrika's upturned face. Then he reached down between her legs, spread open the bruised lips of her pussy with the barrel of his crop, and rubbed it up and down a half dozen times, expertly teasing her swollen clit with the braided leather on each pass.

76

Ulrika screamed wordlessly as she exploded in a huge orgasm. The crop, already shiny with her girl-juice, now was drenched in a downpour of watery cum. She rose up and sank back down on her heels under the direction of Caine's crop, utterly under his control. He continued to excite her long after she was exhausted by the many orgasms and her sexual parts had become unbearably sensitive. Before he was finished, she was weeping and begging him to stop.

"Are you quite certain, my dear?" Caine asked with mock solicitousness. "I thought you *wanted* to come." It was not until she was on the ragged edge of unconsciousness that he finally brought an end to this entertainment.

Ulrika flopped down face-first on the carpet, feeling as if every last bit of energy had been drained from her body. She was still only half-conscious when a pair of servants dressed in the obscene livery of Briarcliff appeared, and dragged her away, back to her basement cell. (Caine's unique uniform for his house servants consisted of a one-piece green spandex body suit with cutouts exposing the buttocks, vagina, and breasts of the wearer, for which reason they were often referred to as "greensuits.")

Caine returned his attention to the trial transcript in the magazine Dane had brought him. He was still reading it when his partner, business manager, and protégé, Quentin Scales, entered the library, sat down in a wing chair facing him, and said "I was told you wanted to see me right away

Mr. Caine. Do you have a new assignment for me?"

This was not mere speculation on his part. Quentin met normally met with Caine daily over either breakfast or dinner, in addition to a weekly business meeting every Freysday, so when he was summoned out of the blue, as in this case, it usually meant that Caine had an assignment for him, the assignment being a trip to an auction to purchase a new slave for his harem.

"No," Caine said. Quentin's eyebrows went up in inquiry. "Not this time," he went on. "I've decided to start a new hobby. I want you to sell off all my fuck-toys, and use the money to buy a herd of goats. I'm going to start making goat cheese. Of course, that includes the three cunts I lent you. Good milkers are pretty expensive, so I'm going to need as much cash as I can realize from the sales." The "three cunts" Caine referred to were Elenora Reilly, Olivia Addison, and Inga Bergqvist, all of whom were slaves given to Quentin by Caine. The three women were deeply in love with Quentin and were his wives in all but the legal sense. However, even though he no longer used them for his sexual needs, Caine still was their legal owner. Quentin also had a fourth slave-wife, the journalist Bryn Matthews, but she was solely Quentin's property, having voluntarily made herself his slave. (See: *By Judicial Decree 12: Commercial Treaty*.)

The stunned Quentin could only manage to croak "Goats?" Caine smiled and nodded his head. Quentin believed that he owed a debt to the older man that he could never repay. Thanks to Caine,

Quentin was now wealthy beyond any dream of avarice, and the heir to Caine's estate, the seventh-largest fortune in the WP. In return, he had privately vowed to devote himself to Caine, and to do whatever his benefactor asked of him, without question or complaint, no matter what it was. So it was only with the greatest reluctance that he could bring himself to protest, even when Caine had ordered him to sell the three women he loved more than life itself. He took a deep breath, cleared his throat, swallowed hard, then hesitantly began, "Ah, Mr. Caine, sir… you know how…um, grateful I am for everything…, ah, you have done…for…for me…" Here he paused, mopped his brow streaming with a handkerchief, and took another deep breath before continuing, "but…,"

Caine's grin widened and he shook his head in wonder. "Quentin, you are loyal, intelligent, efficient, truthful, and conscientious, just to name a few of your excellent qualities. But it is remarkably easy to 'yank your crank,' as I believe the expression goes."

At this, Quentin heaved a great sigh of relief. "I know how much you enjoy your playing little pranks on me, Mr. Caine," he said, "but I would be most grateful if, in the future, you would stick to short-sheeting my bed, slipping a whoopee cushion onto my chair, electrifying the seat of the commode in my bathroom or something else of that kind. If you play another practical joke on me like this one, I might have a heart attack, and I would feel terribly guilty if I left you without a business manager while

I was in the hospital, if I recovered, or the cemetery, if I didn't."

"Well," Caine said, "we can't have that, now can we? Did you really think I would trade in your girls for *goats*? So, the fact that you believed I would confirms a suspicion that's been growing in me for a while now, and it is clear that I have put off something important for far too long. It's past time that I transfer the titles of all three of your women to you, first thing in the morning. Aside from anything else, at the moment Bryn Matthews is the only one you own legally, and I can imagine how her unique status might be a source of... mmm..., friction, let us say, in the bedroom."

"I'm afraid you have put your finger on what I fear is becoming a sore point in my household, Mr. Caine," Quentin answered. "They do their best to hide it from me, but Olivia and Inga are definitely feeling jealous, and even Elenora, the sweetest human being in the world is a little..." He trailed off momentarily. Then he said, "I already owe you so much already, Mr. Caine, so I have no words to express...."

"Think nothing of it, my boy. You've earned it a hundred times over," Caine interrupted. The other man's overwhelming gratitude for what Caine considered to be minor favors such as giving him cast-off slave girls, always made him a little uncomfortable. "However, I would ask you to make Olivia available for my films, if you don't mind." Olivia Addison, one of the first slaves Quentin had bought for Caine, was the biggest star in the erotic films produced by Caine's Mastery Studios.

80

"Of course, Mr. Caine," Quentin answered immediately. "But if you didn't summon me to dispatch me to the monthly livestock auction in King George's Town, you must have had some reason, other than frightening me halfway to a coronary with your little joke, of course. May I assume that I am here because you have your eye on a slave who will be for sale on an auction block somewhere in the not too distant future?"

"Right you are," Caine answered. "As you know, Dane Edberg has standing orders to keep me apprised of any prominent legal enslavement cases." Quentin nodded. Caine slid the magazine he had been reading across the small table between them. "Perhaps you've been following the case yourself."

Quentin picked up the copy of *Notable Trials* and paged through it. Since the entire issue was devoted to the murder trial of Miss Betty of the Wireless Schoolhouse, it did not take him very long to guess the identity of the woman he was being sent to buy. Quentin shook his head. "I'm afraid I'm not familiar with her, Mr. Caine," he answered. "Is she very attractive?"

Caine answered by extending his arm to offer Quentin a second magazine, named *Peek*. Unlike *Notable Trials*, *Peek* contained few words but many pictures, all of photogenic celebrities. This content was evidently irresistible to *Peek*'s readership, which consisted of terminally bored housewives who perused it while waiting in checkout lines at the market.

Quentin leafed through the magazine, stopping when he came upon a photo captioned "The W.P.'s

81

favorite teacher takes a recess." Pictured below was a young woman in dressed in a bathing suit at the beach. At first, he was not especially impressed: certainly, Betty had a very attractive slender, curvaceous shape which the modest one-piece bathing suit did nothing to hide. She had a narrow waist, a solid, upward-inclining bosom, and long, well-tanned legs, but Quentin could see nothing about her physique that was better than (or even as good as) girls Caine already owned, and he very nearly said so.

But then he looked at her face, and hesitated. Betty was smiling back at the camera, and her smile was so filled with innocent fun and cheerfulness, that Quentin found himself involuntarily smiling back. She was the epitome of the charming, friendly girl-next-door who until now, Quentin had considered being no more real than the Loch Ness monster. He knew just from the picture that she was spotlessly clean at all times, took eight showers a day, and brushed after every meal.

But there was something else about her, something that he could not put words to. Possibly it was the roguish way the corners of her lips curled or perhaps her stance, with one foot a little forward and her weight shifted just slightly onto one hip. Quentin did not know why, but he did know that the WP's favorite schoolteacher was giving him a considerable erection, just from looking at her photograph.

"She kind of grows on you, doesn't she?" Caine said, causing Quentin to drop the magazine, and sit up with a start. "That picture had the same effect on me. There's something about her that makes a man want to ravage her, to befoul that innocent, little body, as if …, oh, I don't know…" He trailed off.

"It as if she is both rejecting you and at the same time, tempting you to…" he paused, "…to throw her to the ground and take her, like a caveman." He looked down again at the picture in the magazine, then back at Caine.

"Well put, Quentin," Caine agreed. "And if she has that effect fully clothed, in a magazine photo, what do you guess she'll look like in person, stripped naked on the auction block?"

"I suppose it will be incumbent upon me to find out, Mr. Caine," Quentin replied. "If you would give me the particulars of the auction, I will do my best to insure that you have the opportunity to see her for yourself."

Caine smiled. "Oh, I imagine I'll probably want to do a great deal more than just *see* her," he answered.

Chapter Six: Helmburg

Following the lead of the Federal government, most of the states of the WP sent their valuable judicially enslaved prisoners to one of the big auction houses. In the eastern half of the WP, this usually meant that state slaves were sold at the Celestial County Auction, famed for the quality of its offerings, or occasionally at the Carmen Brothers, in one of the latter's semi-annul premium sales. The advantages of selling at one of the major slave auction houses were several: the sales were widely advertised in advance, the established auction houses attracted more buyers, and they possessed the expertise needed to get the greatest possible return for the slaves they sold.

But the state of Westmark, of which New Stavanger was the capital, was among the handful of that conducted auctions of condemned prisoners in-house. The authorities in these jurisdictions calculated that whatever financial benefit gained from using the big auction houses was lost to the seller's premium, up to 20 percent of the hammer price charged to the sellers. This at least, was the official justification.

That was why Quentin, two weeks after his meeting with Caine, found himself in the auditorium of Helmburg State Prison, a gloomy pile of stone located in the middle of nowhere in rural Westmark. There were perhaps 500 metal folding chairs on the cracked, gray linoleum floor, facing the proscenium stage that was normally used either for religious services for the inmates or dramatic productions by them. There was not, Quentin noted, a single unoccupied seat.

Over the stage, on either side, and at strategic locations around the auditorium, video screens had been set up, so that the attendees who failed to secure a chair, and were therefore consigned to the stand in the overflow area in the back, could see the lots being displayed as they were put on the auction block. Naturally, none of the professional slave agents were subjected to that particular indignity; they had all been provided with seats in the central sections of the first or second rows. Quentin, who represented only one buyer, but that one was the seventh wealthiest man in the country, so he seated dead center in the first row, directly below the auctioneer, where the lots would be shown.

The overhead lights flicked off and then on again, a signal for the loudspeakers on the ceiling and walls to blare to life, and the murmuring of the crowd to cease. "Your attention, please. Your attention, please," the announcer urged. He then rattled an obligatory introduction in a bored monotone. "The annual premium slave auction of the State of Westmark is about to begin. All proceeds will go to a fund to benefit the widows and orphans of employees of the Westmark correctional system who died in the line of duty, so please keep in mind that your money will go to a good cause, and be generous. The State of Westmark thanks you." There was a brief pause before the announcer, his voice now rising in excitement, cried out, "And now presenting your auctioneer for this evening's sale, Mister Blaine Black!"

There was a round of applause when a slender man in a dark suit strolled out from the wing. This was Blaine Black, who was by all odds the most famous slave auctioneer in the WP (and the best in the business, for Quentin's money.) Naturally, his fees were correspondingly high, which seemed to effectively negate the alleged reason for the state to conduct the sale itself, since Black's fee would be as great or greater than what the auction houses would charge. No doubt the true reason was the greater opportunity this method provided for the prison bureaucracy to get a rake-off before what remained of the proceeds finally reached the supposed beneficiaries of the sale, Quentin thought.

The man seated to his left must have been thinking along much the same lines. "I'd be surprised if the widows and orphans end up with ten farthings on the crown," he said cynically. This was Quentin's friend and sometime competitor, the veteran slave agent, Harley Jackson.

"Now don't be so cynical, Harley," Quentin admonished. "Why would you think that a poorly-paid bureaucrat in the State Department of Corrections would go so far as to take advantage of his position by getting a rake-off from a charity?"

"Why? Because I didn't just come from Bumfuck County riding on a shipment of rutabagas, that's why," the other man retorted. Quentin snorted.

"While we're asking questions," he continued, "what could possibly have brought someone as important as the general manager of Caine Enterprises all the way out to this benighted hole?" He gestured contemptuously up at the stage, where Blaine Black was trying to whip up interest on a 30 year old redhead with a decent, if not outstanding, body and the hard-boiled face of an old lag. The woman was a pickpocket, Quentin saw after consulting the auction catalog. She had been sentenced to enslavement as a persistent offender, after multiple convictions for theft. "It wasn't to pick up *that* beauty for Caine, was it?"

Since the lot in question was not physically appealing enough to be a house slave at Briarcliff, Quentin answered, "Right you are, old boy; I have no designs on the fair Mrs. Held." (This was the woman's name.) "She's all yours," he added generously.

Harley glanced up at the stage again, where by some miracle of salesmanship, Blaine Black had contrived to get the bidding up to 450 crowns, then glanced sidelong at Quentin. "No thank you," he answered sourly. "I can get my dog food cheaper back home." Again, this brought an incompletely suppressed snort of laughter from the other man.

"I'm going to take a wild stab in the dark," Harley went on, "and guess that you're here for that fake schoolteacher."

Quentin did not answer immediately, because just at that moment, Blaine Brown slammed his hammer down and cried, "*Sold* for 460 crowns, to Number 127! Congratulations, sir!" As they watched the handler lead the naked redhead away, Quentin said, "You're in the wrong line of work,

Harley. With talent like that, you could be a professional mind-reader. However did you guess?"

The other man rolled his eyes. "Does Caine really need *another* fuck-toy? What does he do with all the other cunts you bought for him: grind them up for library paste? Give them away to charity?" He demanded. "I *knew* I should have skipped this sale and gone to the Carmen Brothers sale, instead of wasting my time coming down here."

Quentin paid no attention to the agent's complaints. His attention was focused on the lot that had just been brought out. Given the overall low quality of offerings in prison auctions, he had not expected to find a girl other than Miss Betty who was worth a second glance. But the girl now standing at Blaine Black's side on the stage was worth a second, and even a third, look.

She had fine, light brown hair, full lips, high cheekbones, a thin, delicate nose, huge dark brown eyes, and was clearly from the upper levels of society. She was wrapped in an air of melancholy that pulled at Quentin's heartstrings. No young girl, particularly one so beautiful, he thought, should be so forlorn, so hopeless.

He tore his eyes away from the stage to read the description of the girl in the auction catalog. Her name, he learned, was Halli Fairbourne, she was 21 years old, and she had been enslaved for the crime of murder. He returned his attention to the stage just in time to see the slave handler pull the bow-knot on the front of her robe, causing her sole garment, the white cotton slave robe to float to the ground, revealing Halli's unadorned, natural form. Quentin, who had seen literally thousands of naked women, many of them notable beauties, stared at her slender, ethereal nudity, transfixed.

Although Halli was only a few inches over five feet tall, her proportions created the illusion of height, as if she was a goddess, towering over mere mortals. Her small, upthrusting breasts, lithe frame, long, smoothly muscled legs, and the uncannily smooth, effortless way she moved, as if gravity did not affect her, all contributed to the overwhelming impression she made on Quentin. "A flower in a dung heap," he muttered to himself.

Harley overheard him. "She wouldn't be too bad," he conceded, as the girl was stripped, "if you put a few pounds on her. She's built too much like a hat rack for my taste?"

Quentin didn't hear him. "Beautiful..." he murmured. Or perhaps the right word was "exquisite," he thought. There was something strange about the way she stared out at the crowd, as if she wasn't even seeing them, how she scarcely seemed to notice when the auctioneer bounced her breasts in his hands, then turned her around to fondle the perfect curves of her buttocks and run one hand into the vale between. Indeed, Halli displayed not a sign of the humiliation one would expect to see, so distracted was she by her grief.

Halli's unusual reaction to being stripped, displayed and handled in front of a crowd of strange men (or rather, the lack of one,) along with her slenderness and smallish breasts, was in Quentin's estimation, why interest in her was lukewarm.

Harley realized that Quentin's interest in the girl was more than casual, when he raised his card to bid on her. "On second thoughts, I can see great potential in this one. I'm sure Caine will be crazy about her. He likes the skinny aristocratic type, doesn't he? " he said, trying to encourage Quentin to buy the girl, in the hope that this purchase might satisfy the other man, and give him a chance at the main prize of the day.

Quentin ignored him, raising his card again to bid 1600 crowns, which turned out to be the hammer price. "So, Quent, old boy," Harley said, after Blaine Black had banged down his gavel to finalize the sale "Does this mean you won't be going after the Wireless Schoolteacher?"

"I'm afraid not, Harley," Quentin answered. "Miss Fairbourne was just an impulse buy. Having too much money can be just as bad a problem as not having enough, in some ways: you can forget the value of a crown," he added philosophically.

"Maybe," Harley answered, "but I'd be willing to risk it, if you want to trade places and return to the carefree life of an independent agent."

Quentin shook his head in mock regret. "You know I'd take you up on that offer in a second if I could, Harley," he said, "but I can't trust anybody else to look after Mr. Caine properly. Now, why don't you stop brooding over the unfairness of the universe and do some work? Take a look at that little redhead they're bringing out now: I guarantee from the way her robe bulges that she's got a set of tits that'll knock your eyes out." He glanced down at his catalog to read the bio information. "She's got a brain too; she was a certified public accountant who caught with her hand in her employer's cookie jar."

Harley looked up to watch her being stripped, and brightened. The girl was 24-years-old, with curling red hair and milky skin, who stood, according to the auction program, was only four feet ten. Her diminutive stature only emphasized her enormous breasts with their wide, red nipples and areola. She was not exactly beautiful, but with her wide, green eyes, snub nose and a sprinkling of freckles on her cheeks, she was certainly charming. In any case, her male admirers would probably not be spending much time looking at her *face*. Harley instantly thought of three very wealthy customers who would drool at the sight of her.

"If you think she's all that, why don't *you* buy her?" Harley asked, still making a show of resentment that he no longer really felt. In any case, he already knew the answer: Caine was not attracted to women with over-large mammaries, like this one (Nor was Quentin: he found that any disproportionate feature, whether it was huge breasts or a long nose, was esthetically unpleasing.) So Quentin never bought any unusually buxom slaves

The agent could not contain his grin, when the little redheaded embezzler went to him for a mere 1000 crowns. This coup restored Harley to his normal, agreeable self. He leaned over closer to Quentin and said, "If I can't get 3500 crowns for her in Jorensburg, I'll turn in my license and do what you said, become a stage magician."

Two hours later, after they were obliged to sit through a seemingly endless parade of lots with short, dumpy legs, prison tattoos, square buttocks, flabby or misshapen breasts (sometimes both,) long noses, piggy eyes, thick, clumsy ankles, and other unattractive physical traits, in short, the usual fare for a prison sale, the final item in the catalog was called.

"All right folks," Blaine Black boomed, "if anybody in the back accidentally dozed off during this exciting sale, it's time to wake him up..." he waited for a little wave of laughter to subside, then continued, "because we have reached the final lot, the one that brought you all here to historic Helmburg Prison. Ladies and gentlemen, the Westmark State Correctional Monthly Slave Auction is pleased to present for sale, the most famous educator in the Western Provinces, the Wireless Schoolteacher herself...," he paused dramatically, then finished, "Miss Betty Carroll."

From stage left came a slave handler wearing the traditional all-black uniform of his profession (the auctioneer's company included professional handlers as part of the package,) with a dark-haired woman in a white slave robe at his side. That part of the stage had intentionally been left in shadows, to make the appearance of the slaves more dramatic by keeping the audience in suspense about what the girls looked like, until they reached the brightly lit display area. Considering the quality of the majority of the offerings, the auctioneers would have done better to have kept the stage in total darkness, so

92

that the lots would be invisible, in Quentin's opinion.

Now he looked up eagerly as Betty Carroll was brought out. He wondered if the photographs were some sort of trick, or if the Wireless Schoolteacher truly possessed that perplexing, compelling aura of a virgin whore both he and Caine had both found so erotic. *I'll know in a few seconds*, he thought.

Chapter Seven: On the Auction Block

She sat on a wooden bench offstage, listening to the auctioneer sing her praises to the crowd who were waiting for her to be stripped naked and sold like a farm animal to some wealthy pervert. She could bear *that* part easily enough, she told herself, since she cared less than nothing about their opinion of her. She had nothing but contempt for the way men could be led around by their insatiable appetites, like so many ringed bulls. *They're nothing but walking sperm dispensers*, she thought, and smiled.

But the smile disappeared when she was once again confronted by cold reality. She was now in thrall to these brainless animals, and worse still, was about to become a sexual plaything for one of them. *How did I let them do this to me*? she demanded silently, and as on the other countless times when she had asked herself this question, there came no answer.

"Pull yourself together!" she muttered fiercely under her breath. "You've got to *think*."

The handler must have thought she had spoken to him. He turned and said in a kindly tone, "Just relax, Ma'am. You'll only be naked for a few seconds, and as soon as it's over, I'll bring you back here, so you can put on your robe again."

She smiled at him and said, "Thank you," in her sweetest virgin schoolteacher voice, suppressing the impulse to add, "...then it's off to start my new career as a fuck-doll!" It would be foolish to antagonize the handler for any number of reasons, beginning with the shock rod in his belt, she realized, but what was more important, she needed her ability to manipulate men more than she ever had before, and for that, she had to be thinking clearly.

I'll start by working on that slavering crowd of idiots out there, she decided, *then on whoever buys me. By the time he gets me home, I'll have the dumb pig wrapped around my little finger.*

She felt a tug on her arm. "Come along, Miss Carroll," the handler said. "We're on."

She walked at his side out to center stage, then she threw up her hands to shade her eyes, when two bright overhead spotlights caught her in their glare, momentarily blinding her. She heard the cheering crowd before she could blink away the colored dots obscuring her vision to see them.

She was looking over a large, dingy room resembling the cafeteria of a slum high school. She estimated that there were at least 500 hundred chairs set up in rows below the proscenium stage, with nary an empty seat in the house. Even the space in the back between the last row of chairs and the wall was full to capacity with the milling crowd of patrons not lucky or quick enough to secure a seat.

Not that they would have been sitting at the moment, anyway. Many of the of the crowd in the had left their chairs to stand up when she appeared, to get a better view of the celebrity slave, and this had obliged anyone else behind them who wanted a glimpse of the Wireless Schoolteacher to do the same. With the exception of the cool-eyed, professional-looking men in the front two rows, practically the entire crowd was on its feet, and they all seemed to be bellowing at maximum volume, making her feel as if she was at the stockyards while a trainload of cattle was being unloaded.

The auctioneer, a slender man in a dark suit was speaking into the microphone on the stand in front of him, but although Betty was standing no more than two feet away from him, she could not make out a single word in the hubbub. However, the overhead speakers were producing audible, if not comprehensible, sounds, and gradually, when they realized the auctioneer was saying something, the din grew less, until the crowd was quiet enough for everyone to hear the man.

While the noise died down, the auctioneer covered the mic with his hand, turned to Betty, and said, "I shouldn't have any problem getting bids on you. It sounds like the animals are shaking the bars of their cages before we even start."

"They sound like a pack of hungry hyaenas," she responded.

The man smiled and winked, "And you're the main course," he agreed. He lifted the hand that was covering the microphone, and addressed the crowd.

"Well, folks, here she is, the one you've all been waiting to see, the famous Wireless Schoolteacher herself, Betty Carroll," he proclaimed. They endorsed this statement so

96

enthusiastically that it took Black another minute to quell the renewed uproar before he could continue.

"Now I'm sure the pretty lady here appreciates all the attention and cheers," he said, when he could be heard again, "but we have business to conduct, and we need to raise some serious money for those widows and orphans of the brave prison guards, and Miss Betty is going to do all she can to help out, aren't you, my dear?" He paused, waiting for her to answer.

Once again, she realized that her first impulse, which was to tell the auctioneer and the crowd to go fuck themselves and raise the money by selling tickets to the event, would be counter-productive, so she left it unspoken. Instead, in her most sincere, softest tones, she answered "Oh, yes of course, I am always glad to help the needy. I have spent my life working with children. My heart goes out to the poor orphans who have no one to love them."

Black smiled down at her, then turned back to the crowd. "Just listen to her, folks! Have you ever heard of such a big-hearted murderer?" The audience responded with a roar of derisive laughter.

"Now," he continued in a more businesslike way, "who wants to see if the schoolmistress's body is as sweet as her voice?"

She could only make out a few of their answers in the uproar that followed, but those few, "Strip her!...Show us her tits!...Let's try her on for size...," and similar sentiments were more than sufficient to satisfy her.

Once again she suppressed the urge to spit her defiance in their faces. Mastering her anger, she turned her head away, closed her eyes, and employing her matchless ability to mimic real emotions, making herself blush in an authentic-looking superb display of profound humiliation. It was all the more remarkable considering that at that moment, she was imagining how pleasant it would be to hose down her auditors with concentrated sulfuric acid.

The auctioneer nodded at the slave handler, signaling the latter to pull the loose end of the bowknot that held the neck of her display robe together. The wide neck opened, and the robe slid down to lay in a pool at her feet, leaving her nude. She now built on her performance, by turning her entire body to one side, covering her breasts and vulva with her hands, and forcing her eyes closed even tighter. She squeezed out a few tears as well, and they glittered like diamonds on her cheeks under the bright spotlight. Had an artist desiring to paint a picture of "The Maiden Forlorn," been present, he would have needed to look no further for his inspiration.

"I thought you said you were going to be *helpful*, Betty," the auctioneer said, shaking his head in disappointment. Speaking slowly with exaggerated precision, as if he was addressing a small child, he continued, "Only bad girls break their promises, and we all know what happens to *them*, don't we?"

Blaine Black looked at the handler and nodded sharply. The big man seized Betty's wrists in one hand, forced her arms behind her back, then lifted her hands high over her head, pulling her up on her toes with effortless strength. In an instant, the crowd was treated to an unobstructed view of her arrogantly jutting breasts, flat belly, rosy-lipped sex and deliciously curved hips. She resisted, trying to pull away from his grip, but it was as if her arms were clamped in a steel vice. The handler was so much stronger than her that he did not appear to notice her struggles as he drew her higher, until she lost contact with the stage, her feet futilely kicking the air. Held this way, it felt to her as if the pressure on her shoulders would dislocate both arms. The pain was blinding.

"Well, if you're not going to cooperate," the auctioneer told her, "we'll just have to go ahead without your help." He signaled the handler by tracing circles in the air with his forefinger. The big man responded by walking back and forth along the stage while turning the helpless Betty to display her nudity to the crowd from all angles.

After he had carried her from one wing of the stage to the other, the handler returned to drop her at Black's feet, at center stage, then stood behind the sobbing girl with his arms crossed over his chest.

The auctioneer tipped her chin up until their eyes met. "Are you ready to cooperate *now*?" he asked.

"Y-yes," she gasped. "What…do you want…me to do?"

"I want you to help out those poor orphans, by letting all those people see what a lovely slave they will be bidding on," he answered. "Now get up, and show off your tits."

Slowly, painfully, she gathered her feet under her, and stood up, with her arms at her sides, looking at her tormentor for further instructions. "Now show these nice people your tits," he ordered. "Arch your back and hold them up so everyone can see how firm they are."

Dutifully, she stiffened her spine, arched her back, and lifted her breasts to display them as instructed. Then she screamed, when Black suddenly seized her hair and pulled her head sharply back, bending her body into an agonizingly tight arc. She instinctively grabbed his hands to protect her scalp, which felt as if it was being torn bodily from her head.

"Put your hands back where they were, Miss Betty," the auctioneer growled, "unless you'd like our friend here to demonstrate how well that shock stick in his belt works."

"I will, but *please* don't pull my hair out!" She cried. She reluctantly returned her hands to her breasts, and once again, displayed them for the avidly watching men. Black did not respond to this plea aloud, but he did loosen his grip on her hair slightly.

"Can any of you honestly say you ever saw a better pair of tits than these, my friends?" Black demanded. Of all the people in the crowd, only Quentin Scales had a reason to hesitate, for he was the owner of Elenora Riley, who he long believed possessed the most beautiful breasts in the world. Looking up at the stage, he was forced to concede that Betty's breasts might be a match for Elenora's in their extraordinary form, firmness and color. Part of the attraction was the striking way the Wireless Schoolteacher's mounds inclined so proudly away from her ribcage. Another part was the delicate pale rose color of her creamy skin, the bright red nipples set in small, virginal rosettes rede on them. Nor could he overlook the superb resilience of the flesh, which Blaine Black displayed by lightly slapping them back and forth, to the crowd's vocal approval.

After holding the naked Betty bent painfully back for perhaps 30 seconds, Black released her hair, and barked, "Now get down on your hands and knees." She immediately dropped to the boards, and crouched at his feet facing the crowd.

"No, no," he admonished. "Turn around and show them your ass. You're not ashamed of your ass, are you, Miss Betty?"

She glanced up at him for an instant, her face frozen, but her eyes burning with hate. *Why don't you show them your ass, and see if anybody wants to fuck you,* she thought, but she was able to swallow her words before she spoke them aloud and made her situation worse (*If that's even possible,* she added mentally.)

Still on all fours, she obediently shuffled around in a semi-circle, until her buttocks faced her auditors. Then she waited, her head down, as demoralized as she had ever been in her life. *At least,* she thought, *I can't sink any lower than this. I'm at rock bottom right now, so there's nowhere to go but up.*

Almost immediately after she had this comforting thought, she saw that she had been wrong; it *was* possible to sink lower, after all. The

101

auctioneer's shadow fell on her as he leaned down to place a hand on her left bottom cheek. He plumped, patted and squeezed the flesh, and said, "If your mouth isn't already watering after those tits, this ass should do the trick. Anyone out there who doesn't want this sweet little virgin warming his bed after seeing her *au natural* should ask your neighbor to check your pulse; you're probably dead might be dead." He paused to give the audience time to appreciate the sight.

Then he resumed putting Betty through her paces. "All right, now you're going to open up your legs and raise your hips so they can see your pussy," he said. He put one shoe in the middle of her back and applied light pressure. "Get your tits down on the floor," he directed.

At last Betty's temper snapped. She was so enraged that she no longer cared what they did to her: she had had enough. She turned her head and opened her mouth to respond with a few selections from her unequaled collections of obscenities. If she had said what was on her mind at that moment, she would have certainly regretted it after the handler had finished punishing her with his control rod. Fortunately for her she never had the chance to speak.

It was at this exact moment that Blaine Black reached the end of the crowd's patience. "Come on! Get on with it," someone in the back bellowed. Like a dam suddenly giving way all at once, this was followed by a positive flood of similar demands from the crowd, creating a deafening uproar when practically everyone in the room was shouting for

Black to start the auction. Confronted with this unexpected revolt, Black responded by surrendering instantly.

He raised his hand, and waited until the crowd had calmed somewhat, then spoke into the microphone again. "It doesn't seem that I have much choice, so I will bow to popular demand, and open the auction." He seized Betty's hair, and pulled her to her feet again in one quick motion.

"Who will open the bidding for this lot at ten thousand? Do I hear ten thousand gold crowns for this superb...? Yes, ten thousand over there. Do I hear eleven? Eleven, eleven, eleven... eleven thousand by the gentleman in the third row..."

The bidding was brisk, and did not begin to slacken until it passed forty-five thousand crowns, which put it out of the reach of all but the handful of slave agents who had been commissioned by some wealthy client to buy the celebrity slave, and of course, Quentin.

He entered the auction at fifty thousand crowns, expecting little competition from the professionals once they were made aware of his interest, since they well understood that his bid meant that none of them had a chance. Since he had become Caine's partner, Quentin had never yet failed to be the high bidder in any auction he had entered.

Surprisingly, a young agent by the name of Jorgensen continued the hopeless fight long after his fellow agents had given up. Each time Quentin bid, he glared in the latter's direction as if he took the older man's bid as a personal insult, then spat out a higher bid. Finally, he recognized the inevitable and threw in the towel, at eighty-five thousand crowns.

"I have eighty-five thousand, eighty-five, down in front," Blaine Black chanted, looking at Jorgensen. "Do I hear ninety?"

The agent glowered at Quentin, looked back up at the auctioneer, gritted his teeth, shook his head and sat down heavily.

"Eighty-five thousand *once*, eighty-five thousand *twice*...," Black banged his gavel down on the sounding block and shouted, "*Sold* to Number Twenty-one, Mr. Quentin Scales, for eighty-five thousand crowns. Mr. Scales, on behalf of the Westmark State Correctional Relief Fund for Widows and Orphans, I want to thank you for your generosity. Let's all give him a hand, shall we?" He asked, clapping his hands. The entire crowd, including the professional slave agents, came to their feet to join in, with the sole exception of Jorgensen, who remained sullenly in his chair with his arms crossed over his chest.

Quentin rose, waved his hand over and bobbed his head to acknowledge them. As he was making his way out, Jorgensen stopped in front of Quentin and said threateningly, "Big deal. Anybody can be a sport with Caine's money. You know, someday an agent is going to get fed up with the way you push us around and feed you a mouthful of knuckles."

Harley jumped up, his fists balled and started towards the other agent. "Now look here, you..." Quentin motioned him back, then smiled easily at Jorgensen. "You know, in my day, the younger men walked a little more softly around veteran agents until they had established themselves." Here his right arm shot out and his big hand closed around the other man's throat. He continued in the same mild tone, while Jorgensen made strange sounds while he clawed futilely at the vise gripping his windpipe and his face reddened. "So let me give you some good advice, young man. You're going have to learn how to control your temper if you intend to remain in this business for very long." With this, he released the now only semi-conscious Jorgensen, while at the same time giving him a slight push, so that the other man fell backward across a pair of folding chairs, which collapsed, dropping him to the floor.

Quentin stood over the fallen Jorgensen, and in the same pleasant tone said, "It's been a pleasure meeting you. Now, if you'll excuse me, I must attend to business." He turned and walked away, as if the other man had ceased to exist.

Chapter Eight: Sin

Quentin went immediately to a room that was normally used as a waiting area for prison visitors. Today it had been co-opted for auction business. He went to one table to pay for his two new chattels, then to another to give the restraints he had brought for them to a guard (he had as usual, brought an extra set of shackles along in the event he made an unanticipated additional purchase,) found a chair, and sat down to wait. He amused himself by watching other buyers pick up their chattels, mentally comparing them to the two slaves he had purchased, and wondering if Halli Fairbourne really was as stunning as she looked when he saw her on the stage, or if he had been imagining things.

Finally, Betty and Halli emerged from the bowels of the old prison followed by a handler holding leashes clipped to their metal collars. Quentin jumped up and went over to them before their escort could ask for him.

"Those two are mine," he called, waving his receipt, as he approached. "Here you are," he said, offering it to the handler. As the man inspected the paper, Quentin inspected the slender brunette, Halli. He sighed invisibly when he saw that the girl truly was as heartbreakingly lovely as he had thought.

"And you're not exactly hard on the eyes either," he muttered to himself, when he gave the dark-haired, dark eyed pseudo-schoolteacher a once-over.

"Hmm? What's that, sir?" The handler asked, passing the receipt back to Quentin.

The latter shook his head. "Nothing," he said. "Talking to myself. You'll find yourself doing it too, when you get to be my age. Now, are they both in the restraints I supplied?"

"Yes, sir," the young handler answered immediately. "I locked 'em on myself. Take a look," he offered. He placed a meaty hand on Halli's shoulder, and spun her around so that her back was to the men. Then he lifted the hem of her robe up to the base of her neck, allowing Quentin to check both the installation of the restraint system, and the girl's trim ankles, long, aristocratic legs, perfect hemispheres of her buttocks, and beautifully muscled back at the same time.

Although the shackles appeared to be properly installed, since he was using a new and somewhat more complicated system, Quentin took a few moments to test for himself. He squatted and slid his hand down Halli's back to the base of her spine then grasped the metal disk where all the cords met, and gave it a sharp tug. Then he ran his hand over the silken flesh of her bottom, along the inside of one warm thigh to her ankle, and tugged the rope that attached to the ring there. By the time he completed his inspection, he had developed a rather inconvenient erection. He unobtrusively adjusted his stiffness to a less uncomfortable position before standing back up again. "Yes," he told the handler, "that's fine. You can drop the robe now."

The girl had not reacted visibly to being displayed and handled. She was still distracted by her private grief to such a degree that he would not have been surprised to learn that she wasn't even aware that she had been sold. He was looking forward to talking to this girl whose suffering he felt so keenly on the train back to Briarcliff. What was her story? How could such a gentle, sad creature possibly have committed so violent a crime?

"The other one's ready, sir," the handler said, interrupting his woolgathering. The man had positioned Betty and pulled her robe up, revealing the back of her somewhat more mature body, with her long, athletic legs, firm oval buttocks, flaring hips and slender waist. Certainly, the Wireless Schoolteacher had physical charms at least the equal of the younger Halli, but for some reason, Quentin was not nearly as tempted to take the opportunity to fondle her. He needed only a brief glance to see that the restraints had been applied with due care, and did not trouble himself with them any further

"Yes, whoever put them on did a professional job," he told the handler. "Thank him for me, will you, please"

"Actually, I installed them myself, sir," the man said somewhat diffidently,

"Very good, indeed," Quentin answered. He pulled out his billfold, and peeled a crisp note from the roll, which he extended to the handler. "Here's a little something for you. I would be much obliged if you could just pass over the controller for the restraints," he went on.

The man accepted the bill and tucked it away in his pocket. When his hand emerged, it was holding a plastic oblong device from his pocket, which he handed to Quentin. He said, "Thank you, sir," turned and started to walk away, pulling the banknote from his pocket, unfolding and examining it as he did. But when he saw the denomination, he stopped short, turned around, held out the bill toward Quentin and said, "Excuse me sir, but I think you made a mistake. This is..."

"Simply my token of appreciation for a job well done," Quentin interrupted with a smile. "It was well earned. Very nice meeting you," He finished, then nodded politely in farewell, to indicate that their business was concluded. The handler hesitated, then shrugged and started back the way he had come, whistling cheerfully.

To the two women, Quentin said, "Face back to me, please. We will be leaving shortly, but before that I have a few things to cover that will help make our journey together more pleasant for us all, so I will need your attention."

Betty responded instantly by leaning toward him, opening her large dark eyes as wide as possible, and fixing an expression on her face that suggested that her entire being was focused on him. Halli's reaction was delayed, but with an obvious effort she tore herself from wherever her mind wandered, and forced herself to join them in the here-and-now.

"First, of all, my name is Quentin Scales," he said, "and I will be taking you back to my home with me."

"It is a pleasure to meet you, Mr. Scales," Betty offered, "and I am glad indeed that we will

109

have such a handsome gentleman with us on the journey." She smiled to show how glad she was. The flattery, he thought, was laid on rather too thickly and her insincerity was, to Quentin, obvious. Halli said nothing, waiting for him to go on.

"Now, I will tell you something about those restraints you are wearing," he continued, ignoring her pleasantry. "They are controlled by this device..." he held up the plastic object the handler had given him, "and with it, I can adjust the ropes to any length I desire. Let me give you a little demonstration of how they work."

He flicked a switch at the top of the remote with his thumb, pointed it at Betty, then pressed a button. A soft whining sound arose from the metal box on her back, and her arms and legs began to slowly draw together. She gave a startled yelp, then fell to her knees, her limbs still being pulled inexorably toward the base of her spine. "Ah!" She cried out, "What's happening to me?"

"There is an electric motor inside that housing on your back," Quentin explained. "Although small, it is as you can see, quite powerful. It is reeling in the ropes attached to your wrists and ankles." He paused, watching until the process was complete and the whine of the motor had ceased. By then Betty was lying helpless and immobile on the floor, her hands and feet gathered together in the small of her back, her body arched back sharply in what amounted to a hog-tie.

"This is what will happen if you attempt to escape, attack me, or are uncooperative," Quentin

110

said, looking sternly down at Betty. "In addition, the restrains can…"

"I understand!" Betty said urgently. "I'll cooperate, I swear it! Please let me up!"

Quentin resumed as if she had spoken. "Nor is this the maximum in discomfort this restraint system can deal out," he said. "It can do the same thing to the cord attached to your collar…," he paused a moment to give the women a chance to imagine how it would feel to have their necks bent backward so sharply, then continued, "…as well as transmit an electric shock. In addition, there is a homing device inside the collar that can be detected from up to five miles away, so even if you somehow overpowered me and escaped, it is a near certainty that you would be speedily recaptured and severely punished. Any questions about any of that?"

"No, no, I understand sir," Betty said, "and you don't have to worry about me. I'll do exactly what you tell me, if you just let me go!" This time, Quentin had no doubts about her sincerity. He nodded, pressed another button, releasing the tension and allowing the cords to spring back to their original lengths.

He had surreptitiously monitored Halli during the demonstration, and saw her eyes widen as she watched what the restrains did to her fellow chattel. He was pleased to note that his demonstration had made an impression on the girl, not that he believed she was any sort of flight risk; but simply because he was glad to see this evidence of an ability to snap out of her private world, if the motivation was sufficient. This meant that she would, given time, almost certainly recover from the damage her mind had suffered.

There being nothing more to detain them, Quentin shook the leashes of his two lovely companions, and directed them out of the prison to the car he had hired, which was waiting at the curb for them. He helped the women into the car, then slipped around Betty to sit between them. Quentin used the two-hour ride to the train station in New Stavanger, where Caine's private railway car awaited them, to become better acquainted with the two sex slaves, both because he considered providing personal information about newly purchased chattels to Caine part of his job, but also because in this particular case, he wanted so badly to comfort the delicate Halli, which he could do only if he knew the circumstances that led to her committing murder. He paid so much attention to her, that he hardly spoke to Betty at all. This did not sit well with the former wireless celebrity, who was accustomed to being the center of male attention at all times.

At first, Halli responded to Quentin's warm, sympathetic conversation with monosyllables and even after he was able to coax entire sentences out of her, she still seemed distant, as if only a small portion of her consciousness was in the car with him, and the rest was somewhere far away. It wasn't until after they had settled down in the Caine's luxurious parlor car for the trip to Briarcliff that she found a way to share her story.

Oddly enough, it was Betty, whose empathy for other human beings was close to nonexistent, who broke through Halli's barriers. She had been growing increasingly irritated by the way the younger girl had been able to virtually monopolize Quentin's attention, as this did not allow her the opportunity to employ her sure-fire techniques for using the brainless rutting instinct of men to attract, then control their new owner (she was not yet aware that she and Halli belonged to Caine, not to the former slave agent.)

She had at first believed that Halli was pretending to be distracted by grief *(or whatever the hell it's supposed to be*, Betty snarled in her thoughts,) for some purpose of her own, perhaps to gain Quentin's sympathy. But eventually she decided that the girl's behavior was genuine, which made Betty even more impatient, until she finally felt as if could not tolerate it for another second.

"That's enough," she burst out, suddenly. As this was the first time she had spoken in over an hour, they stared wide-eyed, in obvious surprise and bewilderment when Betty continued, "I'm sure you found murdering another person traumatic, but just consider how it felt for whoever you killed. You're still alive at least, which is more than he can say. Stop feeling so sorry for yourself, and for the love of Baldur, grow up!"

There followed a period in which the women gazed at each other in silence. At last Halli said with quiet intensity, "Not he, she. My sister."

"What?" Betty asked. "What about your sister?"

"That's who I murdered," Halli answered, "my twin sister, Runa ."

113

On hearing this Betty experienced what was for her an unusual emotion: embarrassment. Halli had murdered her own *sister*, and even Betty see how that could be a hard thing to live with . "Oh," she began, "I didn't know…"

"I loved her," Halli continued as if Betty had not spoken. "I loved her more than life itself, so I gave her the only thing I could, the one thing she wanted in all the world." Crystalline tears formed on the ends of her long eyelashes, as she said, "I gave her the gift of death, and now I must suffer for my sin." By the time she pronounced the word "sin," tears were tracking down her cheeks, over her lips to her chin, from whence they fell unregarded to the floor. The dam had finally burst.

She cried a long time. Quentin went to sit beside her on the sofa, putting his arms around her protectively, while she sobbed softly, her face buried in his shoulder. After a time, she raised her head, and said to Quentin, "Thank you, sir." Then she looked at Betty. "You have it exactly backward, you know. She begged me to kill her…"

***

Halli and Runa were identical twins, and like many siblings who shared a single zygote, they had a special bond. They went everywhere and did everything together while they were growing up, and even after they both began to develop individual interests (dating, for one. Three was *definitely* a crowd on a date,) they still retained an uncanny way of knowing what the other twin was doing when they were apart. So on the night of the accident, Halli knew something terrible had

114

happened long before the call came from the hospital.

"Her boyfriend was driving her home when his car was broadsided by a gasoline truck." Halli said. "He was killed instantly, crushed when the car rolled over. Runa survived, but she was pinned inside the wreck. The car was lying in a pool of gasoline, so when it caught on fire, she couldn't get out..." A passing motorist risked his own life to drag the unconscious Runa out of the wreck, but she had already been burned over 80 percent of her body. The doctors did not expect her to survive until the next morning.

"But they were wrong," Halli said. "She didn't die that night, nor the next, nor the week after that. A month later, she was still alive, floating in a tank of water, because she was too badly burned to be put in a bed. Her fingers and toes were all gone, and where her hands and feet had been were just shriveled stumps. Her hair was all gone, of course, and so was most of her face..."

She stopped and bowed her head, momentarily overcome by the memory. "That's all right," Quentin said, stroking her hair. "You can skip over that part. In fact, maybe you should just stop..."

She instantly raised her head and exclaimed, "But I *can't*! You don't understand; I must tell you everything, so you'll know what a terrible sinner I am." He started to object, but then she added, "Please let me, I beg you," with such desperate intensity, that he shrugged and answered, "All right, if you insist."

115

"Thank you," she said, sighing and relaxing. She picked up the thread of her story. "I visited her at the hospital every day, and we talked. She could still talk with what was left of her mouth, although I don't think anybody but me could understand her. She told me she was in terrible agony every second. At first I thought that as time passed and her flesh healed, she would get some relief from the pain, but that didn't happen. The scar tissue that replaced her skin tended to pucker, and any movement, even the smallest one, would set off another explosion of unbearable pain."

She took a deep breath, looked up at the ceiling, then closed her eyes and lowered her head, as if its weight was too heavy for her slender neck to bear. "She begged me to release her. She felt guilty for asking, because she knew what it would cost me, but she couldn't go on any longer. She told me she wished all day, every day, for death to come for her, that she could think nothing else, and that she would soon go insane from the pain. But I still couldn't do it, I just couldn't." Her voice fell until she was almost inaudible. "Finally, she told me that if I loved her, I would do as she asked, and if I didn't, she never wanted to see me again."

"She knew I couldn't live knowing she hated me." She ran her hand across her eyes to wipe away the tears. "I said, 'All right, I'll do it.' I went to the side of her tank, looked down and whispered, "Good-bye, Runa ." Then …," she stopped again, took a long, shuddering breath and said, "then I put my hand on her forehead, and pushed her poor scarred face down until the water covered her. I held her there for a full minute after the bubbles stopped. When I let go, her face was blue and she wasn't breathing, so I knew she was gone."

She waited fifteen minutes, to make sure there was no chance for Runa to be resuscitated, then picked up the phone and called the police to report the murder she had just committed. She made a complete confession, and when she was brought into court to be arraigned, normally a formality in which the accused invariably pleads "not guilty," she instead tried to plead guilty to Murder in the First Degree. Both the prosecutor and the judge advised her against this, and when she insisted, an attorney was appointed to represent her, and she was ordered to undergo a mental health evaluation.

"When they found I was sane and competent to stand, I was brought back to court, and this time, the judge had no choice but to accept my plea," she continued. "There is a mandatory sentence for Murder in the First Degree...,"

"Yes," Betty said, "I know. But I don't get it. What you did was the kindest thing you could have done, a good thing, a very good one. The court and the prosecutor understood, and anyway, no jury would ever have convicted you. So, why...?"

"I intentionally took a *life*, my own *sister's* life," Halli snarled, her features distorted in a sudden rage. "Don't you understand what that *means*?" Almost as soon as the words left her lips, she subsided and answered her own question. "No, of course you don't. You don't live by the Book of Life, so you don't understand that *debts must be paid*." The last words were spoken, or rather recited, as if they were part of a ritual, which of course, they were.

"I have heard of the Life Church," Quentin said, "but I must admit that I know almost nothing about it, except that the Lifers reputation for fanatical pacifism."

"It is written in the Book of Life that life is a loan to us from the One who is the maker of all things," she explained. "He gave us free will, so we can choose: follow the Way, by helping the unfortunate, the sick, the broken and the defeated, meeting hate with love, and above all, protecting and defending His most precious creation: life; or walk the path of sin. If we repay His loan with good works, in the end our souls will be released from our bodies, to join the One in eternal bliss. But if we misuse our lives, break His Laws and waste what he lent us, our souls will sink under the weight of sin into the Dark Place, to remain there until we have suffered enough to pay off the debt, and release our souls. *Debts must be paid*," she repeated, even more emphatically than before. She raised her hand and made a mystical gesture.

"My soul carries a crushing burden of debt ever since I took poor Runa's life," she said. "The sin is far greater than any credit I could possibly earn in life, and I must spend many thousands of years suffering in the Dark Place before my soul has been cleansed, and the One repaid. Do you understand now?" She asked.

"Not altogether," Quentin answered. "It seems to me that you were motivated by love to perform an act of mercy. I have some difficulty viewing

118

what you did as a 'sin' that deserves punishment at all, let alone thousands of years of suffering. Surely the One understands why you did it and forgives you."

Halli shook her head impatiently. "The Law was made by the One at the beginning of time, and even He is bound by it. It *must* be obeyed, because is part of the very fabric of the universe He created from the primal dust. Mr. Scales, if you fell from a tree while trying to rescue a kitten, would you expect the law of Gravity to understand and give you another chance?" she asked sarcastically. "There is no way to evade the workings of the Law, and no one can avoid the consequences if she breaks it. It is the Law, eternal and impartial: 'So it has been from the Beginning; so it shall be at the End,'" she finished, quoting from the sacred text, as if this settled the matter once and for all.

Quentin looked at Halli speculatively. "So, because the Book of Life says you are going to Hell…excuse me, the Dark Place…, you arranged to be convicted of murder, so you would be enslaved and would start suffering right away," he said, hardly believing it himself. "Do I have that right?"

"Yes, naturally," Halli said. "If I have an unusually harsh master, perhaps I will suffer enough to work five, or even ten thousand years off my debt before I die." She considered the mild-mannered Quentin, and asked, "Are *you* my new owner?" sounding as if she hoped the answer would be "no."

Quentin shook his head in bemusement. This girl with her unusual religious beliefs was

119

something new in his experience. Usually when he told the new chattels about Caine, they begged him to keep them for himself, but in this case… "It so happens that when I purchased you…" he said, then turned to Betty, "…and this applies to you as well, Miss Carroll…, I was acting as an agent for my senior partner, and I will be delivering you to him tomorrow. You both know the name, I think."

"Who is he?" Betty asked.

"He is not infrequently a subject of stories in newspapers, periodicals, and newsreels," Quentin said. "He is most widely known for his film studio, and is said to have the seventh largest private fortune in the Western Provinces. I believe you will find him harsh enough for your purposes, Miss Fairbourne. His name is Rupert Caine."

Upon hearing this name, the blood rushed from Betty's face. Quentin concluded that she had heard of Caine, and what she had heard about him had not been very encouraging. Halli on the other hand, had somehow lived 19 years in the WP without reading or hearing any of the stories about the most notorious billionaire in the country, which Quentin found nothing short of remarkable. She said, "Hmm. I *may* have heard of him, but that's about it. What's he like?"

You'll find out soon enough, Quentin thought. *Mr. Caine will arrange for you to suffer enough to satisfy even* your *god.*

Chapter Nine: A Short Lesson

The car was hooked onto a southbound train car a few hours later. After they were underway, Quentin sat down with the newly purchased chattels to eat the meals he had ordered from the dining car. He kept them both in the restraints , leaving them with their hands bound behind their backs and incapable of feeding themselves. This meant that they were both obliged to wait until after Quentin had finished his meal, then sit patiently while he fed them. He believed this reminded the new slaves of their dependence on the good will of their master, and helped to impress the nature of their status as slaves on them.

Halli gave no indication that being fed like an infant bothered her, but not so Betty. Although she did her best to maintain her sweet kindergarten teacher persona for Quentin's benefit, the humiliating process of being fed like a fledgling bird by its mother caused her to slip up and allow her true feelings to show when she thought he wasn't looking. She did not realize that Quentin, who

He decided to put his suspicions about Betty to the test after dinner. "Miss Carroll," he said, seating himself on the sofa, "Could you come over here, please?"

She obediently rose, walked over to him, and asked, "How can I be of assistance, Mr. Scales?"

"I think I would prefer you address me as Master Quentin, like the other slaves at Briarcliff," he said, then smiled up at her and waited expectantly.

"Ah…yes, of course," Betty answered, her face reddening slightly. "How can I be of assistance to you…" there was a brief hesitation before she added, "Master Quentin?"

"I like you to pull your robe up over your waist," he said, still smiling gently, "then lie down over my lap for a spanking."

Betty's face darkened in anger. "You want me to do *what*?" she snapped. Then, regaining control of herself, she suppressed her rage, and in a much softer tone, said, "I mean, why am I being punished? If I did something wrong, I don't know what it was, but…"

Quentin waved his hand and shook his head. "No, no, you didn't do anything wrong," he told her, "however, this is not a punishment."

"Then what…?" she began.

"It's something Mr. Caine wants me to do with all his new fuck-slaves," he explained, "so I can give him some idea in advance of what to expect from you. Now, if you don't mind…?" He patted his lap to indicate that he wanted her to get into position for the spanking.

She now recalled her degradation on the stage at the hands of Blaine Black and the way she had so meekly submitted to him. Why, she hadn't put up any fight at all; she hadn't even dared to give the sadistic bastard a piece of her mind. *I am not a coward*, she told herself. *Maybe I can't stop him, but I don't have to help him. Anyway, what was he going to do if I refuse to cooperate? Spank me?*

"Well?" Quentin asked.

"Well, nothing," Betty answered. "I'm not doing it. I don't care *what* you call it; I refuse to be punished for no reason. It's unfair and…Ah! Stop!"

While she was haranguing him, Quentin was reaching into his pocket for his remote control. He pointed the device at Betty and pressed a button, and instantly, she felt the remorseless pull of the restraints forcing her hands and feet together behind her. This time it was even worse than when he had demonstrated the device in the prison, because the collar was also retracting, forcing her spine into an increasingly sharp and painful arc. She toppled to the floor at his feet.

"Ah! I can't *breathe*!" Betty screamed. "You're killing me!"

He rose and bent low over her helplessly struggling form to inspect her collar. "No, I don't believe you're in any danger of that," he replied. When she continued to bellow, he went over to a closet and took out a wide roll of tape, then to a dresser, from which he removed a pair of socks. Returning to the caterwauling Betty, he deftly thrust the socks into her open mouth, then sealed them with a swathe of tape over her lips. Her cries, although not completely stifled, were now considerably muted.

He bent over to pick her up, then sat back down on the sofa with Betty sprawled face down across his lap. "You are correct," Quentin said, as he worked her display robe free to expose the smooth, firm flesh of her legs and buttocks, "it is not fair. Sadly for you, that is a fundamental aspect of

123

slavery; there is nothing fair about it. Apparently you need a short lesson in exactly what it means to be a slave."

The tension of the restraint forced her to open her thighs wide, providing Quentin with unobstructed access to the pale ovals of her bottom globes. He ran his hand over her mounds, with a connoisseur's appreciation of their quality. They were resilient, muscular, gracefully curved, with the thinnest layer of padding just below the surface that made it delightfully soft to the touch. Her skin was a delicate shade of coral, as smooth as satin and, he suspected, would be unusually sensitive.

His thoughts became clouded with lust as his hands roved freely over the delicious half-moons spread out over his lap, until he almost forgot why he had put her there. With an effort he forced down the fantasy he had started to weave, in which Betty Carroll was his alone to do with as he pleased, adjusted the uncomfortably stiff erection that had sprouted in his pants and got back to the business at hand.

He raised his hand, then brought it sharply down on her left cheek with a wet *smack* sending Betty into furious, but quite futile motion. The flesh quivered momentarily under the stroke, then returned to smooth rotundity, but now it bore the imprint of five fingers and the palm of his hand in red. "Miss Carroll," he said patiently, "I'm certain you know this already, but I will remind you that you are a slave, animate property without rights of any kind. I do not *need* a reason to 'punish' you, any more than I needed to ask permission of this sofa to sit on it."

He spanked her a dozen more times, until both of her globes cheeks were blotched by overlapping red marks, then paused to examine his work. "Believe me or not as you please, but I am actually doing you a favor," he said. Betty twisted her neck around as far as she could to look at him. "This spanking would not even rate as a gentle reminder from Mr. Caine," he explained. "If you spoke to him the way you just to me, he would..." Quentin paused, momentarily trying to imagine what sort of punishment Caine hand out to a slave who was insubordinate, disobedient, and disrespectful all at the same time. "Now that I think about it, I don't know *what* he would do, but I do know that whatever it was, you would remember it to end of your life, which might very well be that same day."

He reached down between her legs, then gently spread the lips of her sex to investigate the state of the interior. Betty resisted the in the only way she could, by wiggling her hips. Quentin immediately put an end to that. He slapped her buttocks so hard that it sounded like a gunshot, and made her entire body jerk in reaction. "Stop that, unless you want another ten," he growled. She reluctantly subsided, and did not attempt to resist while he conducted an intimate examination of her body.

First, he checked for the presence of a hymen. He felt reasonably certain he would find one, based on the auction which stated that she was a virgin. Of course, it was not uncommon for true virgins to lack a hymen, but in such cases the auction house would not make that claim, as it would be impossible to prove the matter one way or the other.

Sure enough, an inch or so inside her lower lips, his finger encountered a little scrap of tissue obstructing the entrance to her vagina. Next, he performed the most important part of this inspection, examining her state of arousal (or the lack thereof.) He was not surprised when he discovered the slippery goo of her natural lubricant, and a clitoris that was as hard as a jujube, but neither had he expected it. After a lifetime of examining the private parts of young women, Quentin had concluded that it was impossible to predict how any particular slave girl would react to bondage and mild discipline until she had experienced it. Some (more than one might think) were aroused by it, while it left others cold.

Not that it mattered to Caine. After he trained a slave, she was all but incapable of achieving an orgasm without some preliminary bondage and flagellation, no matter how she had reacted initially. Also, they generally had learned to enjoy orgasms *a lot*, and they would go to great lengths for one. *It's a strange thing when you think about it*, he mused. *He even dominated a woman with a will of iron who also happened to be a life-long lesbian, turning her into his submissive sex-toy.* (For all the particulars, see *By Judicial Decree 9: Court Martial*. CJB)

Betty made a desperate high -pitched noise, and writhed like a snake on his lap, snapping Quentin out of his reverie. When he looked down, he realized that while he had been lost on the back roads of his mind, he had been continuing to absent-

126

mindedly roll her clit in his fingers, and had quite unintentionally excited her to the point of madness. Betty's hips were churning in ardent spirals, reproducing the motions of the hand controlling her stiff love button. Her face was red and covered with perspiration, her eyes wild with need.

"*Mmmmm!*" she demanded, her eyes fixed on his with laser-like intensity, as if she was trying to communicate by telepathy, then repeated, "*Mmmmm!*" Whatever her speech lacked in clarity was compensated for by intensity.

"Oh, yes…, er…please accept my apologies, " Quentin stammered, embarrassed by his unprofessional conduct. He hastily withdrew his hand. "I had no intention …"

Betty whined again, then rolled her eyes at the hand he had just pulled from her sex, his fingertips greasy with her juices.

"Oh, of course. You want me to finish you, I suppose," Quentin said.

She nodded as far as the collar would permit and moaned, "*Ehhhhh!*"

"Certainly," he answered, returning his hand to her sex. Experimentally, he ran the side of his forefinger lightly up and down over the stiff, slippery bulb of her clit. "How's this?" he asked.

Betty squeezed her eyelids shut, grimaced, and exclaimed, "*Urrrrr!*" Since becoming Caine's right-hand man, Quentin had from personal experience, become an expert at interpreting speech as distorted by a gag, and was thus able to correctly interpret this apparently meaningless noise as "Harder!" He obligingly applied more pressure, while also increasing the pace. Betty ground her pelvis down on his hand, moving her hips faster and faster until she exploded, crying out in wordless ecstasy, and soaking his hand, trousers and the sofa with a discharge of fluid.

Afterward, Quentin stood up, laid Betty on the sofa, and used his remote control to reset the restraints to their normal setting. He wiped his hand with a handkerchief, glanced down briefly at the stain on his trousers and shook his head. He reached out to slowly pull the tape from her lips then held out his hand to receive the sodden socks she pushed out of her mouth with her tongue. She glared at him, and started to tell him what she thought of the way he had handled her while she was tied up and helpless, but stopped with her mouth open when he shook his head and tapped the pocket of his jacket that held the remote control.

"It's clear you do not properly appreciate the favor I just did for you, which comes as no surprise," he said. "Be that as it may, our relative status has not changed: you are still a slave under my supervision, and what you like or dislike carries less weight than last year's mouse dropping. I apologized because I failed to meet my own standards as a professional agent, *not* because of anything I did to you."

When she continued to glower at him, he sighed and shook his head again. "Well, it's plain that you aren't interested in anything I have to say, and as I don't feel like having you glare at me all evening, I think the best thing for everybody will be to clean you up and get you to bed," he said. Before she could voice any objections to this plan, he added, "We can do it with you gagged or not. It's your choice."

"*Not*," she muttered sullenly, standing up and starting toward the bathroom followed by Quentin.

He opened the bow-knot to strip off the robe, then directed her into the shower. He removed his own clothing, making sure she saw him place the hand set for her bonds on a shelf next to the shower stall, then turned on the taps. He plucked a scrub brush from a hook inside the shower stall, and began to ply it over her gleaming, wet flesh. Showering naked with a beautiful, naked woman had the effect one might expect, and Quentin would normally have normally enlisted the aid of the new chattel in tending to the consequent erection (*not* by copulating with her, to be sure, as this was a breach of the slave agent code,) with a session of mutual masturbation

But this time, even though his organ was almost painfully erect, he made no further effort to fondle or sexually excite Betty, confining himself to the cleaning process. Oddly enough, she did not show any sign of gratitude for his self-restraint. Indeed, Quentin suspected that she was, at least in part, disappointed..

Neither spoke until after he had put her robe back in place and they had returned to the parlor, when Quentin unlocked a cabinet, brought out a hypodermic needle, and said, "Come over here." He pulled open a panel to let down a bed, patted the mattress and gestured with the needle. "Just lie down here, and I'll put you out for the night with this. It's a sedative."

"How do I know what that stuff is?" Betty asked, not moving. "For all I know, it could be poison."

"How do you know?" he repeated impatiently. "Because I just told you, that's how. If you would rather do without, I can make the cords tight again, put my socks back in your mouth and leave you trussed and gagged all night. So make up your mind, Miss Carroll. What'll it be?"

"All right, all right, I'll take the shot," she said grumpily. She went over to the bed and stretched herself out on it, eyeing the needle suspiciously. "Be careful with that thing. I'm very ...ouch!" She started, then yelped when Quentin jammed the point into her thigh and pressed the plunger home.

"I told...you to...be...careful...." she said, each word coming more slowly, until she trailed off into silence as the powerful sedative carried her off into deep slumber. Quentin hooked a short safety line to the junction box on her back, so that she would not roll out of the bed in her sleep and injure herself.

He stood over her and thought: *You have a lot to learn, Betty Carroll, and Mr. Caine is not a gentle teacher. I almost feel sorry for you... Almost.* Halli had remained a silent observer while he was occupied with Betty. She had been silent so long that he had all but forgotten she was there. He was forcibly reminded of her existence, when she asked, "So, aren't you going to spank me too? Mr. Caine will also want to know how *I* react, too...won't he? "

130

Quentin spun around to face her. "I suppose so," he answered. "Would you feel cheated, if I didn't do it?"

"What a strange thing to ask!" Halli remarked. "I'm sure I heard you tell Miss Carroll that what a slave wants is of no consequence, 'no more than last year's mouse droppings,' was the way you put it, I believe."

"I did indeed," he agreed. "So why don't you come over and get over my lap for your spanking." As she settled herself over his thighs, he said, "By the way, I strongly suggest that you start addressing me as 'Master Quentin,' just to get into the habit. Mr. Caine is a stickler for that sort of thing, and he will punish you if you forget."

"Thank you for the advice...," she hesitated for a fraction of a second, then added, "...Master Quentin." She lifted her hips to make it easier for him to slip the hem of her robe up over her hips to expose her buttocks. "Should I call *him*, 'Master- whatever- his- first name' is, too?"

"No, no, *no*!" Quentin responded, slapping Halli's naked buttocks emphatically, and drawing a yelp. "That would be a *very* bad idea. *Nobody* addresses Mr. Caine by his first name. He is a private sort of person, and he does not tolerate over-familiarity, especially from his slaves. He *does* permit a few of his favorites to call him 'Mr. Caine,' 'sir,' or 'boss,' but *never* his first name."

"Understood, Master Quentin," she replied. "Once more, I am in your debt." She glanced back over her shoulder. "So, when are you going to start...Master?" she added.

After administering the one slap, Quentin had left his hand where it had landed, and while he was explaining the proper way to address Caine, he had been, sliding his hand up, down and over the satiny flesh, enjoying the sensation.. Although the erection he had developed while spanking Betty had afterward subsided, the urges she had excited were still unrelieved. He was not surprised to feel a new, even more insistent stand grow as he handled the young Lifer. Her bottom-cheeks felt as good as Betty's had, and had a slight edge in the perfection of their curves.

Her question reminded him of what he was supposed to be doing, again. *I wonder if I'm becoming absent-minded?* he thought. *I'll have to ask the girls when I get back to Briarcliff.*

"I'm starting... *now!*" he announced, raising his hand high, and bringing it down again hard, making a sound as loud as a gunshot, and marking the place the blow landed with a red handprint. Halli's entire body tensed from the effort of stifling her cry of pain. Even so, a soft "Ah!" escaped.

He waited until her *gluteus maximus* relaxed again, then immediately struck twice without a pause, once on each cheek. Halli seemed to have gotten the measure of the pain from the first stroke, Quentin concluded, because this time, she did not cry out. He spanked her eight more times, alternating between hemispheres. When he paused to inspect the results, he saw that the girl's buttocks were an even brighter shade of red than Betty's had been, and the flesh was warm to the touch. Also, although she had been able to remain more or less silent throughout, her legs had pounded the floor in a lively, impromptu jig. She was also unintentionally rubbing and pressing her remarkably flexible midsection on his trousers at the exact place where the tip of his turgid organ was pressing against the cloth, which only made it harder and Quentin less comfortable. He took a few moments to adjust his clothing, maneuvering his rod into a somewhat less awkward position in his pants. "May I...ask a ques...question, Master...Quentin?" Halli panted, as he did.

"Certainly, my dear girl," he answered without looking up. "You may ask *me* whatever you like, but I must warn you not to ask Mr. Caine any questions without permission. I should tell you that his slaves are not permitted to speak to him at all, unless they are spoken to first, and it would be wise to remember that rule. Now, what is your question?"

"Thank you again, Master," she said. "Well, it looked to me as if you aroused Miss Carroll when spanked her. Do you expect the same from me?"

Now he looked up and she returned his gaze, looking impossibly young and naive. He shrugged. "I have no expectations one way or the other," he said. "It really doesn't matter in the long run. The way Mr. Caine trains you..." He was stopped by the picture of this delicate girl in Caine's dungeon that popped unbidden into his mind.

"That's enough talk for now," he said. "Let's finish this, so I can get you showered and in bed."

He resumed the spanking, but although the blows on her already reddened bottom stung, she

133

could tell that they were not as hard as before. His heart just did not seem to be in it.

After a desultory half-dozen additional spanks, Quentin slipped his hand up between her thighs. Halli obligingly opened her legs to allow him to probe her sex, then patiently remained still while he spread open her lower lips and teased her love button. She displayed not the least sign of discomfort during this intimate examination, which had Quentin shaking his head again. On the other hand, neither did she show any indication of arousal after his expert manipulation, so after five futile minutes he gave up. *This girl*, he thought, *is something new to me*.

"Just a waste of time," he said briskly, rising from the couch and helping her to her feet. "Let's get washed up and into bed." He opened the drawstring at the neck of her robe, and slid it down over her shoulders.

"Are you terribly disappointed, Master Quentin?" Halli asked. He glanced at her suspiciously, thinking she was mocking him, but one look at her guileless face told him otherwise. "I'm sure I could do better, if I put my mind to it," she continued. "Maybe you could try me again after the shower."

He smiled ruefully down at her, but did not reply. "I'll adjust the water while you take care of your personal needs," he said, indicating the commode. When she was ready, Quentin stepped aside to let her into the shower stall, then stood outside watching the water flow over her lovely, young nudity. Usually on these occasions, he liked to strip and get in with the new girl to help her to reach places where the bondage made it impossible, but he didn't particularly feel like it tonight. Halli's odd behavior and bizarre beliefs had dampened his interest at a time when he normally would have been unable to keep his hands off her, particularly after he had been left high and dry by Betty Carroll.

"Say, Master Quentin," Halli called, breaking into his gloomy thoughts, "could you help me out, here?" She gestured with a sponge at her lower legs. "I can't..."

"Yes, of course," he said, rousing himself, and going over to take the sponge. When she turned to hand it to him, the movement sent a miniature cascade from the open shower directly at him. Quentin jumped back, but not in time to save his trousers from being splattered.

"Oh my!" Halli exclaimed. "I'm so sorry, Master. I didn't mean it."

Quentin studied her face. She would have looked convincingly innocent, but for the roguish twinkle in her eyes. He frowned and thought about telling her she was getting another spanking as soon as she got out of the shower, then stopped, looked down at his pants and laughed.

"Yes," he agreed, "a most unfortunate *accident*. I suppose I'll just have to take off my pants, and while I'm at it, I might as well strip down and get in there with you." He matched his words with deeds, slipping out of his clothing and hanging it on a towel rack. In a few seconds, he was as naked as Halli and sporting an unconcealed erection.

The girl was plainly not put off by the sight, if her warm smile meant anything. She turned to present her back to him for cleaning, while craning her neck around, so she could continue to look at him. "*Most* unfortunate," she repeated. When he began to ply the sponge over her calves, she said, "Just a *little* higher please, if you don't mind...," then sighed when he guided the sponge over the inflamed flesh of her buttocks. "*Ah*, that feels good, Master. Thank you."

Quentin found the hand holding the sponge had somehow wandered up her back, over her shoulder, and down the other side, there to shuttle back and forth from one firm, young breast to the other, making the stiff nipples bend and spring up again like little antennae with each passage. His other hand had found its way around to her smooth abdomen, where Halli had taken custody of it and directed it to the lips of her lightly-furred sex.

Quentin did not know whether he was pulling her closer or holding on while she pressed against him, but however it happened, Quentin's turgid rod ended up in the canyon between her fine bottom cheeks, imprisoned in a bed of slippery, wet girl flesh, with the dark red head peeking out from the upper end of the valley.

"How's that feel?" Halli whispered, her lips an inch away from his ear.

"It...uh...it's quite...nice...," Quentin stammered. When she started to stroke him with liquid motions of her pelvis, he seized her by the hips to pull her closer and encourage the movement. Soon, he felt delicate fingers close around the shaft of his cock, pumping it, while her open lips met his and she thrust her eager tongue into his mouth.

Under this kind of stimulation, particularly after he had been left hanging by Betty, it did not require more than a few strokes before Quentin mumbled something into Halli's mouth and came, shooting streamers of goo from his pulsing cock onto her lower back, to be instantly washed away by the shower.

"Master," she whispered, "did you like that?"

"Yes," he answered, as he gnawed gently on her earlobe, "yes, it was very nice."

"I'm glad," she said. Her hand took one on his, and drew it down to the cleft at the junction of her thighs. "Do you think you could you take care of me?"

"It will be my pleasure," Quentin said. His fingers separated her engorged lower lips, and plunged inside, then began a reciprocating vertical motion, with the edge of his hand pressing down harder as it rode over the stiff little button at the top of her sex. His hand moved faster and faster, and this was matched by the lithe movements of her pelvis, until suddenly she cried out, clutched Quentin's hand in hers to press it ardently against her girlhood, and closed her eyes. When she climaxed, her body seemed to melt against his. The soft, throat-bound sounds of her climax went on for a long time.

After they had dried off and dressed, Quentin opened Halli's bed, and they sat down there side by side. "Do you mind if I ask *you* a question?" he said.

"Not at all, Master," she answered. "But even if I did, I'd have to answer anyway, since I'm your slave."

"Well, there is that," he conceded. "This is what I find confusing: you are a devotee of what seems to be a very strict sect. Isn't that sort of thing we did in the shower forbidden? Weren't you violating your Law?"

She laughed merrily, a sound like silver bells. "If you were not my Master, and it would be disrespectful to say so, I would call that silly," she answered. "The One made our bodies so that when we make love, we experience the ultimate pleasure, so he surely must have expected us to enjoy it as often as we could. Why would he set a desire for something so deeply in us, then forbid us from doing what nature demanded?"

Quentin rubbed his chin thoughtfully. "That philosophy is so sensible, I wonder why so few other faiths adopt it," he said. "In fact, I can't think of another one that encourages pre-marital intercourse."

"I don't want you to get the wrong idea, Master Quentin," she said. "The Church of Life does not encourage us to couple with random strangers or over-indulge in *any* pleasure; we are not self-indulgent sensualists. We make love only when we wish, with partners who share our desire. I remember how gentle my father was, the first time I..."

"What?" Quentin blurted, sitting bolt upright and turning to stare at her. "Did you just say that you and your father...," He stopped.

138

"That he was my first lover?" she finished for him. "I knew him longer and trusted him more than any other man, and I knew that he would never hurt me. Who could I trust without reservation, if not him?"

"But...your *father*..." Quentin repeated.

Halli said, "We are familiar with some of the strange sexual taboos of non-believers, including this one, so we do not talk about our practices with them, to avoid persecution. I have long wished to ask one of you, however: what *exactly* do you think is wrong with it?"

He answered immediately, "Inbreeding, of course! The children..."

Halli smiled and shook her head. "We are not ignorant of modern contraceptive methods, Master Quentin, " she said. "I would say that we are far more careful about such things than the general public. In any case, you must know that only a tiny fraction of sexual activity is for reproduction. Let me ask you this: how often do you fuck because you want to impregnate your partner?"

"Never," he admitted. "But I wonder if you are free to make such a decision. If your father wants you , are you in any position to say 'no'?"

This time, she laughed aloud, then hastily apologized when she saw him redden in anger or embarrassment. "Oh, I'm sorry Master," she said, covering her mouth to suppress some residual merriment, "it's just that a professional slave agent saying *that* struck me as funny."

Quentin stared at her stonily for a few seconds, then grinned. "Yeah, I guess it does sound pretty stupid, especially coming from me," he admitted.

"Anyway," she went on, "my father didn't have a thing to do with my decision. I went to him, and we talked everything over before he agreed to do even the simplest thing. Before he finally penetrated me, we spent months getting ready. I had to ask him a half-dozen times before he finally agreed to do it just after my 18th birthday. After that, my sister wouldn't leave the poor man in peace until he broke her in too."

After that, Quentin changed the subject, asking Halli about her school, friends and interests for another hour. At 10 o'clock, Quentin injected her with the sedative, and after she fell asleep, called Caine to tell him what he had learned about the new slaves. Then he undressed and climbed into bed.

Although he was tired, he lay awake for a long time, unable to stop from thinking about the delicate, young beauty, Halli Fairbourne, who was so intelligent and rational, but who accepted so much on faith. He tried his best to imagine what Caine might do to a slave who *wanted* to be punished, but failed. Finally, exhausted by the effort, he toppled into the welcoming blackness of sleep.

Chapter Ten: Introductions

Early the next morning, the train arrived at Caine's private station, where the car was detached and left on the siding, and the train continued south to King George's Town. Quentin dressed his two charges in their slave robes, after first securing their wrists behind their backs with soft cords.

Naturally, Betty had an objection. She was not a "morning person," and was in a foul mood after being roused out of bed at six o'clock. This undoubtedly accounted for her failure to adopt the Sweet Schoolteacher persona and allowing her real personality to show.

"What's this for?" she demanded, pulling away from Quentin when he tried to fit the cords on her wrists. "You don't need...Oww!" she screamed, when he caught a hank of her long, black hair, and pulled her head back sharply.

"Stand still, and let me put these on, or I'll tighten up the restraints in back until you can't move, then put this on," Quentin snapped. "You keep forgetting that owners are not required to explain their actions to slaves, but since you will not be my problem after today, I will tell you why I am doing this. After I tie your wrists, I will remove the other restraints, because this is how Mr. Caine wants you presented. Does that satisfy your curiosity?"

Betty was forcibly reminded of her slip. If she intended to seduce Caine, she realized that she needed to put her Wireless Schoolteacher persona in place.

"Oh! Oh my!" she exclaimed. "I don't know *what* came over me, sir. I beg your pardon for my inexcusable behavior this morning. Please proceed." She lay still and held out her wrists for him.

"Mr. Caine, as I have said, is not the forgiving kind," Quentin told her as he bent over to fasten the new restraint on Betty's wrists and release the old ones, removing everything but the collar. "Play your little games with me if you like, but don't expect them to work on him." He stood when he finished, then gestured for Halli to lie face down on the table next to Betty.

Betty rolled over, fixed her big blue eyes on Quentin, made her most innocent face and asked, "Why, whatever do you mean, Master Quentin?"

Quentin paused with his hand on the metal box of Halli's restraints, glanced at her, and answered cryptically, "I suppose you'll just have to find out for yourself," then returned to what he had been doing.

He directed Caine's new toys out of the rail car and onto the platform. Briarcliff station was a miniature copy of New Guild Station in King George's Town in perfect detail, down to the hexagonal spires, many gables, oddly-shaped windows and faceted crystal lamps. Waiting beside the building in the parking lot was a long, black limousine, whose driver, a female, was standing at attention by its side.

When they stepped down from the train, the driver rushed up on the platform, ignoring Betty and

142

Halli, to take Quentin's sole piece of luggage, a leather valise. "Did you have a good trip, Master?" she asked. "Yes, it went quite well, Emerald," Quentin answered

Emerald was dressed in a simple black cap and a one-piece, form-fitting body-suit made of flexible, green material that glittered in a thousand places under the bright sunshine. It fit the driver, a young, pretty, wide-hipped African girl, like a sausage, and this would by itself have probably gotten the wearer arrested had she worn it on the streets of any city in the WP. But the fit was the least obscene aspect of it. The truly outrageous parts of the driver's garment were the ones that were not there: the cloth had been cut away to expose Emerald's buttocks and pubic delta (which was shaven or depilated, but were in any case, hairless,) as well as her upper thighs and breasts. In addition, this last was both squeezed together at the sides and uplifted by a built-in support, making the driver's not unusually large endowment look far bigger than her measurements would indicate.

The women followed Quentin and the driver to the car, waited for the driver to put his bag in the trunk, then open the door for him, then slid into the passenger compartment. Betty noted that the driver, so solicitous of Quentin, all but ignored both her and Halli. This she took to be a sign of the status of fuck-toys in Caine's household, new ones, at any rate, and filed that information away for the future. What was really on her mind…

Halli evidently was wondering the same thing. "Permission to ask a question, Master," she said.

143

Quentin nodded. "Go ahead," he said.

"The driver's…umm, outfit, " she began hesitantly. "Will we be…"

"Wearing that?" Quentin finished for her. "No, no. That is the livery of the house slaves. Mr. Caine designed it himself. It is not worn by the bed slaves."

"That's a relief," Betty said. "It's positively obscene. So, what *will* we be wearing? Not these rags, I hope." She tugged on her robe to indicate the "rags.'

Quentin considered reminding her that she was forbidden to speak to a master without permission, then decided that Caine would take care of such lapses soon enough. His lips slightly pursed in disapproval, he said, "Nothing, mostly. Mr. Caine believes that clothing is a privilege for bed slaves, something that must be earned. After today, you will both be naked until you have made adequate progress in attitude and mastery of the skills he expects you to learn."

"I'd rather be naked than walk around in public looking like that," Betty muttered under her breath.

"May I ask *another* question, Master?" Halli said.

"Certainly," he said. "Fire away."

"Those marks on the driver's breasts and thighs…" she paused.

"From a whip, yes," Quentin finished. "Mr. Caine follows a program of regular discipline for *all* of his slaves. He is a strong believer in the precept, 'Spare the whip, spoil the slave,'" and I can assure you that you will not find any spoiled slaves at

144

Briarcliff." After this, silence fell for a time, as the two passengers considered the implications of this statement.

They had been traveling down a two-lane road, with a brick wall on the right and open fields bordered by a split-rail fence on the other side. Upon reaching a massive iron gate set in the wall, it slowed, turned and passed through the gate, then proceeded up a road that wound its way toward the top of a hill.

"Welcome to Briarcliff," Quentin said. The two women gazed in awe at Caine's estate, home of the fabled gardens of Briarcliff. They passed an elaborate box-hedge maze, an oval reflecting pool backed by an elaborate fountain that shot streamers of water high into the blue sky, masses of flowers in a bewildering variety of colors that seemed to go on to infinity, a glass-roofed, miniature, marble palace of a greenhouse, and a great deal more that they had no time to take in.

"Odin's beard!" Betty exclaimed. "How much did it cost to build all this? I can't even imagine how much just the maintenance is."

"Not as much as you might think," Quentin said. "The gardens are open to the public year-round, free of charge, and in return Mr. Caine receives a substantial tax credit from the county and the state." He pointed. "Look over on the left and you can see the house."

The car had been traveling uphill ever since it entered the estate, and now a building came into view on the summit. A few seconds later, the limousine turned into a semi-circular drive and

145

pulled to a stop in front of the mansion, a two-story red brick building. The house was built on the same scale as the gardens: it was enormous, stretching away an unguessable distance to the left and right.

The driver jumped out to open the door for Quentin, leaving his two lovely companions to shimmy their way across the back seat to get out. He clipped leashes to the backs of their collars, then directed them up a few steps to a pair of elaborately carved, monumental doors made of some dark wood, the imposing main entrance to Briarwood. The doors swung silently open as they approached (*A good thing too, what with my hands tied behind my back*, Betty thought. *I don't think I could open a door that big with my nose*.)

Waiting inside were a pair of Caine's house servants, who were immediately identifiable by their green cut-out livery. One of the young women was tall and slender, with a cap of curly red hair that was cut to just above her ears on the sides, and to the nape of her neck in back. She had pale green eyes, pale skin with a few freckles and small neat, conical breasts. Her companion was short, perhaps an inch over five feet, with straight, shoulder-length platinum-blonde hair, piercing blue eyes, round, solid breasts, and a sexy, curvaceous shape. They moved into position next to the new girls, the redhead at Betty's left, and the blonde on Halli's right.

"Good morning, Master Quentin," the redhead said. "Welcome home." The little blonde said, "It seems you had a successful trip, Master."

146

"Good morning, Erin," Quentin said to the redhead, as they proceeded down the hallway together. To the other servant, he said, "I'll leave that judgment to Mr. Caine, Tatiana."

The floor was a mosaic of agate, jade, lapis, topaz, and other semi-precious stones that ran the length of the hall. Twenty feet overhead was a succession of pointed arches forming a ribbed vault, making the two women feel as if they had entered a royal palace or great temple. On both walls hung oil paintings, and between them glass niches containing *objects d'art* of gold, silver, ivory and other substances, many encrusted with gems, a fantastic display of wealth.

"You own half of this...Master?" Betty whispered. Stimulated by greed, her ever-active mind was already turning over a thousand ideas for seducing and gaining control over one of her owners, and thereby getting her hands on this fabulous estate.

"In a legal sense, yes, I suppose I do," he said, "but as long as Mr. Caine is alive, I consider it to belong solely to him. Why do you ask?"

"Oh, no special reason," she answered, casually.

Halli made a soft sound, an incompletely suppressed snort of derision.

"What was that?" Quentin asked.

"Nothing," she replied.

"Out with it, Halli," he said. "That's an order."

"Well, if it's an *order*...," Halli said. "I just thought it was funny, Betty pretending she wasn't scheming to get Caine's money." She turned to the other woman. "What could you possibly offer a man who already has a harem of slaves, all of whom are at least as beautiful as either one of us?" She addressed Quentin again. "I am right, aren't I Master? About Mr. Caine's other fuck-toys, I mean."

"You are," Quentin answered, "but how did you know?"

"Because you bought them for him, just like you bought us," she responded. "You obviously can recognize a beautiful woman when you see one, and you have unlimited funds, so there's no reason for you to settle for anything less than the best."

Betty, who had begun to redden in anger after being laughed at, now stared at Halli with newfound respect at this demonstration of her deductive powers. "That's smart thinking," she remarked. "I wish you'd been my lawyer; you might've gotten me off."

When a splash of golden light came into view ahead, Quentin stopped and put a hand on the shoulder of each of his two charges to bring them to a halt. "Mr. Caine is waiting for you up there," he said, his voice serious, his face grave, "and after I introduce you, you will be his exclusively, and neither I nor anyone else will intercede on your behalf if he is displeased with you in any way. I advise you to do your *very best* to make Mr. Caine happy. Furthermore, I must warn you that he is very difficult to please." He looked at them in turn, holding each one's gaze for a long second, before finishing, "Do you understand?"

148

Impressed by his seriousness, Halli and Betty both immediately answered, "Yes, yes Master."

"Good," he said. He turned on his heel, and resumed walking, followed closely by the four women.

The walls of the corridor fell away, when they entered a big open space, brightly illuminated by sunlight pouring in from skylights high above. The room was furnished like an old and exclusive private club, with comfortable-looking leather chairs and sofas, low wooden tables inlaid with mother-of-pearl designs and large, intricate and fabulously valuable handmade rugs from Khalistan underfoot.

Sitting in a brown wingchair, reading a book, was a man with dark hair turning to gray around the temples. As they approached, he put his glasses aside on a small table, carefully marked his place with what appeared to be a hundred-crown note, put the book down next to the reading glasses, and looked up. As there were no other candidates in sight, Betty concluded that this was Caine.

She saw nothing remarkable about the man, at first. He had a straight nose, a strong chin with a small dimple, and crow's feet around his eyes. He seemed to be much like the many older men she and Lars Forsberg had mulcted back in her younger days. For the briefest of moments, she considered the possibility that the stories she had heard about Caine and Quentin's dire warnings were exaggerations, if not outright falsehoods.

Then their eyes met, and in that instant, she knew: the stories were true, all of them. Caine's

149

eyes, black and impenetrable as obsidian, were as warm as a winter night in Antarctica. She knew, somehow, from that single glance, that this was a man who knew everything there was to know about inflicting pain. Betty saw the corners of his lips turn up in what was technically a smile, although it looked more like the expression on the muzzle of a tiger about to devour its prey. She shuddered.

Caine rose from his chair, and came over to meet the new arrivals. "It's good to see you home, Quentin, as always. The hunter returns, triumphant," he observed, his eyes flicking over the two new slaves, "and with an unexpected catch." He approached Halli, and ran his fingers lightly over her cheek. "I honestly don't know how you find them, my boy. Now, why don't you introduce me to these charming young people, so you can get back to your sex-starved harem? I'm sure they've cooked up something special to celebrate your return."

"Mr. Caine, please meet Betty Carroll and Halli Fairbourne," Quentin said, coming forward to stand between them.

"My pleasure, I'm sure," Caine said, "but not as much as it's going to be." He looked at Betty, who flinched. Addressing Quentin, he said, "They look good enough to eat. Thank you, my boy. As usual, you have exceeded my expectations. Now run along, and I'll see you at dinner."

"Yes, sir," Quentin answered. "Goodbye, Halli, Betty. I'm sure I'll see you again sometime soon." He turned and walked away. The two women turned their heads to watch him go, then whipped their heads back around to look at Caine, when he said, "Quentin is a very nice man, don't you agree?"

Without waiting for an answer, he went on, "Now I, on the other hand, have never, to my knowledge been called 'a nice man,' for good reason."

He pulled the string on Betty's robe, opening the wide neck, and causing the garment to flutter to the ground at her feet. He smiled again as he made a leisurely visual inspection of her nudity. She shivered under his gaze. To Betty, this was far worse than being shown naked at the auction. The crowd had only seen her exterior, but it felt as if Caine's eyes were stripping the very flesh from her bones, as if her most secret thoughts were exposed to him.

When he reached up to take her breasts in his hands, she could not control the impulse to avoid him, and she moved back a half-step. Caine shook his head, as if disappointed, then came close and drove his fist into her midsection, setting off a sunburst of pain and driving all the air from her lungs. She doubled over in agony and toppled slowly to the floor.

"When I want to touch you," he explained as he stood over her, "you must let me do as I please. You are my slave, and that means that you are obliged to do what I tell you," he added patiently, as if he was addressing a child. "Do you understand that, or do I need to explain it in simpler terms?"

Betty looked up at Caine, her eyes bulging from the effort of trying to get her lungs to operate again. Her lips moved, but no sound came out. She silently

151

mouthed "*I can't breathe*." Caine had long practice at reading lips, so he had no difficulty understanding.

"Don't worry, you'll start again soon enough," he remarked, unsympathetically. He toed her ribs with the point of his shoe. "You still haven't answered my question. Do you or do you not understand, that as my slave, I expect you to obey me?"

With a desperate effort, she forced her frozen diaphragm and lungs to operate enough to draw in a shallow breath, then croaked, "Yes...I...und..." before the lack of air obliged her to stop with the final word incomplete.

Caine nodded. "I can see that it is a difficult concept for you to master, but I strongly advise you to remember it in the future," he said. "The next time I need to remind you, I will do something unpleasant to you, to help fix the idea in your mind. Now get up, so I can feel your tits."

As she sat up, and gathered her legs underneath, Betty wondered what Caine's idea of "unpleasant" might be, then decided that she would rather not know after all. Slowly, painfully, she sat up, gathered her legs beneath her and got back on her feet, then stood motionless, slightly bent forward at the waist (she had not yet recovered sufficiently to be able to stand straight) while Caine handled her breasts, rubbing the nipples with the palms of his hands.

"When he called me last night, Quentin said you showed some indications of being responsive to mild bondage and spanking," Caine said

152

conversationally. He flicked Betty's nipples, which had stiffened under his touch, and added, "As usual, he knew what he was talking about." He stepped back, raised his hand and snapped his fingers. "All right, that's enough for now. We'll continue this downstairs."

A moment later, another of the green-clad house servants appeared. She was tall and slender with wavy black hair, limpid dark eyes and full lips. She would have been beautiful if not for her prominent aquiline nose. The new servant snapped to attention in front of Caine. "Yes, Master?" She asked. She spoke perfectly comprehensible Anglish, despite her slight accent.

"Patriza," Caine said, "you and Tatiana will escort Miss Carroll here down to Room 1. I think it's time for you to learn the ropes around here, so you will tie her up according to these instructions, while Tatania supervises." He handed her a folded piece of paper. "I'm sure you'll have no trouble learning the routine. All right?"

"*Si signore*...," errr... Master," Patriza responded instantly, raising her right arm in a salute, then stopping halfway in evident confusion. She reddened. "Mi scusi..., ah... my apologies, Master Caine. It is not so simple a thing to forget ten years in the *Regio Esercito*."

"Don't worry, Patriza," Caine assured her. "You can salute me, if that's easier for you. As long as you get the job done, you'll hear no complaints from me."

To the other house slave, he said, "I ordered *her* to get Miss Carroll ready, but I will hold *you*

153

accountable if the work is not done to my satisfaction. Do you understand, Tatania?"

"Yes, Master, I believe I do," she answered cautiously.

"Let us hope so," Caine said. "If not, I'll need to schedule you for another discipline session immediately." He motioned with his chin in dismissal, and said, "Take her away. Room One."

The house servants took up positions flanking Betty, seized her elbows, and marched her rapidly away toward an arch that opened on a stairway. Caine watched them until they passed through the arch and disappeared from view, then turned his attention back to Halli.

"Now, let's see what sort of surprise Quentin has brought me," he said, smiling. He reached for the string of her robe. Unlike Betty Carroll, when her robe slid down to expose her nakedness, Halli did not flinch or display any other sign of discomfort. Instead, she stood calmly under Caine's inspection, apparently at ease.

"My, my, my, aren't you the cool customer?" he said, reaching out to capture her firm breasts. Holding them from below, he ran the palms of his hands over her nipples, then caught the little nubs at the base of his fingers, to squeeze and twist them from side to side. "It's not unusual for a new slave to *pretend* she isn't afraid of me, but they have been, every last one, even Colonel Jo Langstrom, the famous war hero. Either you're the first girl to fool me, or you're actually *not* afraid. So, which one is it?"

154

"I would never try to deceive you, Master," Halli answered. "So I guess I'm not afraid of you. Should I be?"

"Well," he said judiciously, "if our places were reversed, I wouldn't be *afraid*; I'd be terrified. So why aren't you?" He abruptly balled his hands into fists, clamping down on her now swollen nipples, then raised his hands and turned his wrists sharply, pulling Halli up on her toes, and drawing a cry of pain from her.

Halli did her best to answer while Caine held her up in this brutal grip. "*Ah...ah...*I d-don't...uhh...don't know...*ooh*...Master," she gasped. "I could...ahh...try harder, if...you like."

Caine released her, and she gratefully sank down to replace her heels on the carpet. "'You could *try harder*?'" He repeated. "You mean you could *pretend* to be afraid of me?" He bent low over her until their noses were almost touching, and scowled ferociously. "How *dare* you...?" he growled in a tone that, when used to address to his servants, invariably made them pale in fear. Then he stopped, snorted, threw back his head and laughed unrestrainedly.

"I don't see any point in making a bigger fool of myself than is absolutely necessary," he told her, grinning. "You're just not afraid of big, bad Master Caine, and that's all there is to it. Maybe I'll be able to make more of an impression on you, after we've spent some quality time together downstairs."

He raised his hand overhead, and like a jack-in-the-box, another house slave seemed to pop up out of nowhere. She had shoulder-length blonde hair worn in a pony tail, fair skin and large breasts that the Briarcliff livery turned into a spectacular display. Her facial expression was as stern as that of Caine's other house slaves, but Halli thought she detected a glint of kindliness in her pale blue eyes.

"Yes, Master," the newcomer said, straightening up to her full five feet and seven inches, "how may I be of service today?"

"Lorna, this is Halli Fairbourne," he gestured. "She is new to Briarcliff, and I have no doubt she will want to get a good long look at our famous slave-training facilities." He looked at Halli, "Even if she doesn't, she's going to anyway." He picked up a pen from a side table, and wrote something on a memo pad, then tore off the sheet and handed it to the blonde house slave. "Here's what I want you to do with her, Lorna," he said. "Any questions?"

The greensuit's brow wrinkled with concentration as she read Caine's directions, her lips moving. "No, Master," she answered at last. "She'll be set up just the way you wrote it down."

"I have no doubts about it," Caine said. "Put her in Room One..." then immediately corrected himself. "No, Miss Carroll's in there, isn't she? Room Two, please."

"Yes sir, Master Caine," the green-clad servant answered, taking up a position next to Halli. "Come with us, sweetie," Lorna said, and they marched away together, with Lorna firmly gripping Halli's elbow. Caine watched until they passed through the arch to the stairway through which Betty Carroll and her escorts had passed a few minutes before.

156

"An interesting problem," Caine muttered. Perhaps, he thought, a little research would help him to better understand this girl's unusual psychology. He rubbed the top of his head, trying to remember the name of the Halli's holy book, then clapped his hands together explosively and announced, "The Book of Life, that's it." He strode rapidly off in the direction of Briarcliff's main library.

Chapter Eleven: Participation

Caine found the volume he sought without any difficulty, and sat down to read it. Thirty minutes later, he closed the book, rose and left the library. He went across the hall, then passed under an arch, down a flight of stairs to the basement and along the passageway until he came to the door of Room Two. Unlocking the door with the key that hung on a peg outside, he entered the room, and flicked on the lights.

The first thing that greeted his eyes was the blindfolded, naked Halli, with her legs spread wide apart to display the delicate pink lips of her sex mound with its decoration of a few feathery, light-brown hairs. She was on her back, in a position that Caine judged to be as uncomfortable as it was vulnerable. Her head and hands were secured by a triple set of metal rings locked around her neck and wrists respectively, and was obliged to keep her back arched up high to avoid contact with the metal hurdle set three feet below. Her entire body was glittering with droplets of sweat produced by the effort of staying above the bar.

As Caine watched, she momentarily weakened and sank down until her back made contact with the crossbar. This set off a sharp scream accompanied by a shower of sparks from the place her flesh had touched the electrified metal bar, and she instantly snapped back into position again.

Caine strolled over to stand next to the girl, where he reached down to run his hand lightly over her breasts. "Hello, my dear," he said. "How are you coming along? Is the punishment all you hoped for? If not, I'm sure I could come up with something more painful that would meet your expectations."

"I thank…you for the kind…offer, Master," she panted, "but I think…this is quite…, quite sufficient, for now."

"Good, good," Caine murmured. He moved his hand over the silken flesh of her abdomen, and down between her legs to cup her sex. As he spoke, he inserted two fingers in her pussy and began moving them gently about. "Quentin told me a little about your religion, and I thought it might be useful to understand something about your belief system and how it may motivate your actions, so I stopped off at one of my libraries to read up on the Church of Life."

"What did you think of it, Master?" Halli asked. "Are you considering joining us?"

Caine was now running his finger over her clitoris, but despite his expert handling, the interior of her slot was only slightly damp, and neither the lips of her vulva nor her clit were showing any sign of arousal. "As to that, I can't say," he answered. "I would need to do considerably more research before I made any such decision. However, what I *do* know leads me to believe that your church allows you considerable latitude to indulge in sexual activities, and according to Quentin, you have not been backward in taking advantage. But perhaps I was mistaken about that."

"No," Halli answered. "What you said is true. I have had some experience with sex, although not anything like you, I'm sure, Master," she added modestly, "and I liked it very much, as a matter of fact."

Caine did not respond immediately. He knelt between her thighs and vigorously applied his lips and tongue to her sex for several minutes. When he arose, he was shaking his head. He wiped his mouth with a handkerchief and said, "Then I must admit that I am mystified by your reactions, or to be more precise, your lack of them. After many years of research and practical experimentation, I am one of the leading experts in the entire country on the subject of the female sexual response. This is not based on an inflated ego, or at least not solely on that; it is also the opinion of the National Institute of Sexual Research, of which I am a Fellow. Therefore, cannot understand why I am failing to excite you sexually with the same techniques that have heretofore invariably proven successful."

He stood over her, hands on hips, frowning. "Well, I can see I'll have to use stronger measures." He turned away from her, and went over to a cabinet, from which he removed a small tube of ointment, then returned. "This is something I use when training slaves with a higher than usual arousal threshold, like yourself," Caine said, holding up the tube for Halli to see. "I have found that it increases the sensitivity of female erectile tissue, and has reduced the toughest bitches to a state of puling supplication, begging me to fuck them." He continued to talk as he squeezed out a small quantity of the cream on his fingers, then stooped low to spread the lips of her pussy open, capture her clitoris, and rub in the aphrodisiac by twirling the bit of flesh between his fingertips. "I will be very much surprised if it fails to produce similar results this time."

In a very short time, less than a minute, it appeared that Caine's prediction had been borne out. Halli's hips began to make an increasingly ardent series of turns, swinging back and forth in supple motions that followed Caine's fingers, as if she was a machine and her sex knob the steering control. "You feel *that* all right, don't you?" he asked.

"Y-yes, Master," she stuttered. "It…it's very…powerful."

Caine spread ointment on both hands, then seized Halli's nipples, to work the slippery gel into the pink flesh, tugging, squeezing and pinching, until they swelled with blood, expanded and became as resilient as two bits of India rubber. "And here?" he asked, increasing the pressure and rolling the stiff buttons back and forth in his fingers.

"*Ahh*…yes…, yes M-master," Halli panted. "It feels…feels very…*uhh*…" She trailed off, then after a short pause, asked vaguely, "Wh-what was the…the question again…, please?"

"Forget it. It's clear this works, anyway," he said, resuming his manipulations of her clit. For a little while, he silently watched her writhe through a series of remarkable contortions under expert handling, feeling his cock grow stiffer by the second. When he judged that she was at the very

161

edge of exploding, he snatched his hand away, and waited for her to do what every other slave he had ever trained had done in this situation: beg for him to finish her. Whatever the problem was before, Caine was now confident that this girl could be controlled by the same methods that had tamed a police officer, a war hero, a dominatrix and every other woman who had passed in the dungeons of Briarcliff over many years.

But to his lasting astonishment, she said nothing. Her body briefly arched up higher in an involuntary physical reaction, before subsiding, she panted for air and displayed the other typical signs of frustrated arousal for a little while, but soon, after Caine had released her turgid love button, Halli resumed the original position, bent uncomfortably over the electrified bar, and remained there, as if nothing had changed.

"No," Caine said, "I don't believe it." He inserted his fingers in her sex and found the formerly copious lubrication had diminished noticeably, and her clit was now perhaps half as stiff as it had been only a few moments before. He stared at Halli, his lips compressed to a bloodless line, his forehead furrowed. "That cream has never failed to work...*never*," he repeated. "As far as I know, and I know as much as anybody about it, no female with normally functioning sexual organs is physically able to control the effect on her body. So how is it possible for *you*, when Colonel Jo Langstrom, the toughest woman on the planet, could not?" He demanded.

162

"It's very simple, Master," Halli explained. "Since I'm not involved in the act, it's impossible for me to get aroused."

"What the hell does *that* mean?" Caine snapped.

"I mean that when you use my body as a...what was the term ...?" she hesitated momentarily, then continued, "Oh yes, a 'fuck toy,' that's it. When you use me like a toy, a mechanical pleasure device, my mind isn't engaged, you see, I just sort of sit back and watch what's going on, like it was a movie. So, the second you stop physically stimulating me, I just, well..., lose interest."

Upon hearing this, Caine became so enraged that he was momentarily at a loss for words. He purpled and scowled ferociously at the bound, naked girl who dared to defy him as no slave had ever done before. He had to take took several deep breaths before he was rational enough to speak again.

"I can't decide exactly what to do with you," he said. "An untrained slave, a mere slip of a girl tells me that she won't respond to the way I do things, and that I am supposed to let *her* tell *me* how to go about my business. Perhaps you can advise me: should I roast you alive over a slow flame, feature you in an all-day hanging, or simply have you ground up, feet first, then spread to fertilize my hydrangeas. Which do you think is the most appropriate?"

"If I may, Master," she answered, "I would choose 'none of the above.' Before you turn me into fertilizer, may I please explain myself a little more?"

"I can't imagine anything you say can say would change my mind, but go ahead, I'm listening," Caine said.

"Master," Halli said, "I understand what you expect from your slaves, and I want to give you as much pleasure as the others do..."

"Could have fooled me," Caine interjected.

Ignoring the interruption, she went on with great earnestness, "Despite what you may think, the idea of bondage, flagellation, forced orgasms, and all the rest sounds rather exciting. Ever since I read my first B & D novel, I thought it was very sexy, and I wanted to try it myself, but I never found the right partner...until now."

"You're talking about that idiotic fake bondage that's become so fashionable since that stupid book was published... what was the title? *Ninety Shades of Pink*, something like that. They pretend to be master and slave, and think they're so *daring*, with their fur handcuffs and safe words. *Safe* word," he repeated, making it sound like an obscenity. "If the slave can end the discipline whenever she wants, it's just a game of play-pretend, and a foolish one, at that. So, if that's what you want ..."

"Oh no, Master Caine," Halli said hurriedly. "I agree with you, 100 percent. If the slave is running the show, then she's not your slave, and you're not her master."

"Well then," Caine asked, "what exactly do you have in mind?"

"I just want to participate, that's all," she assured him. "I wouldn't dream of trying to take over. Here's what I'd like to try, Master, if it meets with your approval, of course…"

***

After completing Halli's new restraint, Caine stepped back to examine his work. He nodded, satisfied that he had her restrained exactly as planned. As *they* had planned, to be precise. And wasn't that a strange word to use in this context, he thought.

At first, he had been skeptical. After all, what could a teenage girl with absolutely no experience in bondage know about the kinds of sex that Caine enjoyed? But almost against his will, he found himself becoming more and more interested, so that by the end, they were working out the details together.

Halli was wearing a tall leather collar that obliged her to keep her chin tilted upwards if she wished to breathe. Her hands were cuffed, and the cuffs were clipped to the sides of this collar. There was a wide strip of blue cloth tape covering her eyes. Although the object was not visible, she was effectively muted by the long rubbery artificial cock that filled her oral cavity and pressed against the back of her throat (it was, in point of fact, an exact replica of Caine's organ.) This had been inserted through a ring gag that held her jaws obscenely wide apart. As she was unable to close her mouth to even the slightest degree, she was helpless to control the saliva that dripped out to hang down

165

from her chin in long, silvery strands and spangled the soft pink flesh of her breasts and abdomen.

She was standing, her bare feet on the cold cement floor. A rope that descended from a spool on the ceiling overhead was knotted through an eye in the back of the leather collar had enough slack to ensure that the pressure did not inhibit her breathing any more than the collar already did, but was taut enough to keep her upright. Invisible to the naked eye, but no less effective for that, were a pair of wax plugs in her ears which rendered her deaf. Caine had settled this point to his satisfaction when, after inserting the plugs, he stood next to the blindfolded girl and clapped his hands sharply together an inch away from her ear, and she did not startle or even stir. She was (at this point it should hardly be necessary to say it) wearing the standard uniform for a slave-in-training in a Briarcliff dungeon, which is to say: nothing.

"It is quite a good design," Caine told the oblivious Halli, "particularly for a beginner like you. But I still am not completely clear why you believe you will find this sexually arousing, when my bondage did nothing for you."

Standing behind the girl, he reached to take her nipples in his fingers. They were already rubbery when he touched them, then almost instantly stiffened until they felt as hard as a pair of pebbles. Caine chuckled as he twirled the swollen knobs and said aloud, "But then, who am I to argue with success? I've forgotten the first rule of human sexuality: the most important sexual organ is the brain."

He toyed with Halli's engorged nipples for a while, until her body began to undulate in response to each tug and twist. Deciding that she was now sufficiently excited for the next step, he released her, went over to a cabinet, opened the door, and selected two of the implements that were hanging inside, on hooks. He brought these back and laid one aside on a table, while retaining the other in his hand. The latter was a whip consisting of three one-foot-long broad blades of soft leather set in a wooden handle. Each of these blades had metal balls embedded near the tip. The impact of the wide leather stung and reddened the skin especially when applied to delicate areas, while the metal balls inflicted painful bruises, all without risking cuts, scars or permanent marks of any sort. Caine had designed it himself, and he now began to employ it on the part of Halli's body it had been designed for.

"Brace yourself," he advised as he drew back his arm. "This may sting a little." He swung sidearm, slashing her breasts, scoring on her stiffened, sensitive nipples, and making her firm mounds smack wetly together. Halli screamed, a sound that was only barely audible to Caine, who was only a foot away, and twisted like a mad thing, causing her breasts to jounce excitingly.

Caine was so pleased with the result of this stroke that he nearly surrendered to the urge to deliver another dozen. "No," he told the air, "that would be fun, but that wasn't the plan. Anyway, I can always whip your tits later," he added.

The plan had been Halli's. She suggested that she be rendered deaf, dumb and blind, bound, then

167

have Caine tell her what he wanted her to do non-verbally. She would not be able to ask him any questions or respond in any way other than with movements of her body. She and could not even (Caine particularly liked this) beg for mercy.

He dropped the 3-bladed flogger on the table, exchanging it for what he had left there: a riding crop. This was one of Caine's favorite disciplinary instruments. The core was a stiff rod of titanium alloy encased in braided leather. At the tip was a little leather bag weighted with lead shot to provide a solid punch. He would never consider using such a brutal instrument on the breasts of an expensive bed-slave slave, at least not on one intended to keep. But he considered it ideal for most other parts of the female anatomy.

"Now let's see how you like *this*," he said. He snapped the crop down to strike her back three times in quick succession: first, in the hollow just above her buttocks, then midway up her spine, then finally, squarely between the shoulder blades. He was obliged to pull her head back by the hair to hold her in place for the last two strokes, after the first one launched her into a foot-drumming dance of pain.

After the third stroke had been delivered, Caine stood back and waited for her agonized motion to stop, so he could attempt to communicate with her non-verbally. He nodded in approval when she arched her back to present her pert breasts more prominently. Then he applied the crop again, this time tapping Halli between her between the shoulders as both encouragement and warning.

168

Halli instantly took the hint. The muscles of her back corded, as she strained to see how far out she could thrust her superb mammaries.

Caine reached unconsciously for his pants, shoving the head of his straining cock into a less uncomfortable position. It was not the first time he had seen a naked, beautiful young woman posed this way, nor the hundredth time. Nor could he truthfully say that this one was the most beautiful he had ever seen; all Caine's fuck-slaves were at least as beautiful as the young Lifer, and some more. Still, for reasons he could not name, he was as aroused as he had ever been in his life.

Standing before her, he once again captured her nipples in his fingers. They felt as hard as marbles when he pinched them, and nodded. He judged that Halli was even more aroused now. Caine now increased the pressure on the swollen nubs, digging his fingernails into the flesh to obtain an unshakeable grip, then pulled up sharply with both hands.

Halli shrieked with all the power in her lungs, producing a faint "Eeeee!" and instinctively twisted her torso, trying to pull away. Bound as she was, she had no chance to escape, so that her struggles transformed the sharp pain in her nipples to blinding agony. Each movement felt the way she imagined lightning bolts striking her nipples would. She forced herself to remain stationary, clenching her jaws and sinking her teeth into the gag.

"You appear to be in considerable distress," Caine observed, still holding her nipples high enough to force her up on her toes. "Try to think of the positives. You are undoubtedly earning massive credits with the One up in Heaven, or whatever you call it. Before we're done here, you'll have worked off, oh, I don't know..., five hundred years, at least." It is questionable whether Halli would have taken comfort from this, but the question was moot in any event, since she could not hear a single word of it.

"But enough of these preliminaries," Caine said. He released her aching breasts, allowing her heels to drop back down to the floor. He detached the line from the back of the collar, then seized her left ear in a vise-like grip, and led her across the room, stopping in front of a wooden pillory. This was a sturdy three by a three-foot square of oak, divided into upper and lower halves that were joined by a hinge on one side and a lock on the other. There were three holes: the large one, roughly six inches in diameter, was in the center, flanked by the two 3-inch holes.

Caine flipped the top open, then drew Halli down to her knees in front of the pillory. He pulled her head forward, until her neck was resting in the lower half of the large hole, then swung up the other half and locked it, leaving her head on one side and her body on the other. Halli turned her head this way and that, trying to discover by feel what new bondage she had been placed in. Her hands, naturally, were still immobilized behind her back by Caine's shoulder-dislocating harness.

Caine had foresightedly brought the riding crop along. He now proceeded to deliver three heavy blows to the back of each of Halli's thighs with it, starting from just above the knees and ending at the base of the buttock on each side. This was intended as an order for her to straighten her legs and raise her ass. Once again, again gave her time to regain control of her lower limbs, waiting for her involuntary jig of pain to end, to see if she understood the message of the strokes.

"Smart girl!" he exclaimed, when she shakily assumed the desired position, standing with her legs at full extension and arching her back in a spine-crushing curve to present her bottom as high as her anatomy allowed. "But, there's still one more little detail," he said. Bending close over her, and taking careful aim, he swept the crop down to score the soft flesh on the insides of her thighs, just below her pubic delta. Halli made another stifled yelp, a soft sound like "*uuhhh*!" and jumped six inches off the floor.

She had no more difficulty deciphering Caine's meaning this time, and was soon posing with her feet three feet apart, offering Caine an unmatched view of the red lips of her sex and the winking brown asterisk of her anus. Caine was not backward in taking full advantage of Halli's complete submission. He stepped up close behind her, cupping her sex with one hand, then probing inside her sheath with his forefinger. Judging by the quantity of lubrication she was producing, the distended condition of her lower lips and clit, and the way her entire body quivered after the lightest touch, Caine estimated that the girl was very close to an eruption.

He opened his belt, unbuttoned his trousers, and disentangled his erection from his shorts, then shoved everything to the floor. He laid the shaft of his stiff cock in the valley between her bottom cheeks. The flesh was marvelously smooth and deliciously warm and soft. Moreover, Halli was so excited that she compressed his rod delightfully with her fine buttocks, trying to communicate that desperately she wanted him to fuck her.

He understood her immediately, which was, however, not the same thing as agreeing to do what she wanted. "I suppose horniness has driven everything else out of your tiny brain," Caine said. "Otherwise, you would remember what I told you just a few minutes ago: *you* do not decide when or if you will come; *I* do." He drew back a step, picked up the crop which he had left within easy reach, and began flailing the defenseless girl who bowed before him with it.

"You… come…when…I… say…so…, not…before," he said, punctuating each word with a heavy blow of the steel rod. Although he had not forgotten that Halli could not hear a single word of this correction, he believed that she could sense his thought with some subtler, non-auditory sense. This time it took longer for her to regain control of her body, end her mad, bottom waving dance and return to the original position. It took so long that Caine, who was sporting a sizeable erection, tired of waiting.

Under normal circumstances, a slave's failure to resume a position within a reasonable period ("reasonable" being defined solely by Caine, of

172

course,) would earn an additional punishment. In this case, since Halli could not be told why she was being punished, he was inclined to make an exception. Then again, she wasn't going anywhere, and he could always review her misconduct while applying the crop or some other instrument later. No doubt the insistent demands of his almost painfully erect cock added weight to the scales as well.

But whatever the mental process he employed, in the end Caine decided that he would not delay his gratification any longer. He pressed close behind Halli and took a firm hold of her hips, forcibly bringing her frantic motion to a halt. Then he grasped his cock in his hand, and pressed it up to the entrance to her sex, inserted just the tip and moved it up and down, spreading her tumescent labia apart. Halli responded instantly, mirroring the motion of his rod thrusting backward with her pelvis in a desperate effort to impale herself on him.

Once again, this was a violation of Caine's normal rule, that fuck toy was to follow his lead exclusively and never to take the initiative during intercourse. However, the unique nature of this experiment prevented Caine from imparting the standard warning on the subject and, as he had not thought to mention it before they began, he could not in all fairness, hold her responsible for disobeying a rule she had never heard of. At least, this is what he told himself. He did not stop to consider the fact that he had never before applied the concept of "fairness" to his dealings with his slaves, so clouded with lust was his mind at that particular moment.

He dug his fingers deep into her flesh, so deeply that the resulting bruises were still visible a week later, then roared like a lion and rammed his cock into her pussy with a single violent thrust, burying himself to the root. Halli pressed back to meet him just as energetically, making a muffled *"urrrr"* of passion deep in her throat that Caine, preoccupied with his pleasure to a previously unequaled degree, did not even hear.

The walls of her pussy contracted rhythmically on him, an exquisite sensation for Caine, and despite his best efforts to delay the moment, he came almost instantly, something that had not happened since he was in his teens. And now a third rule went by the boards, when Halli, no more able to contain herself than Caine, erupted in an overwhelming orgasm without permission from the master, and Caine did not see fit to correct her, either at that moment (which admittedly, would have been all but impossible,) or later.

This was not simply a lapse of memory by Caine. He could long afterwards recall the first time he had sexual intercourse with Halli Fairbourne in microscopic detail, indeed, he never forgot. But whenever he began to think about punishing her blatant disregard for what he considered to be a most important rule, he would start to smile at the memory, and decided that orgasm control wasn't the most important thing in the world, after all. This happened just after they had both finished coming, and the sweat-drenched Caine was draped Halli's perspiration-slicked back.

He reached around the pillory to pull out her earplugs, waited until his pulse and respirations had slowed enough for coherent speech, then panted, "Yes…, I think that…that went…pretty well."

Chapter Twelve: Surprise

At length, Caine arose. He picked up a telephone and called for house slaves to come downstairs to release Halli and take her to a suite on the main floor. Then he dressed, left the room and walked down the hall to the next room. He unlocked the massive door, pushed it open and went inside.

Uncomfortably mounted on a wooden horse was the straining, nude body of Betty Carroll. Caine stopped to inspect her. He was pleased to see that she had been bound exactly according to his directions by the new girl. She was astride a sawhorse, impaled by the rubbery dildo in her anus, straining to stand up on her toes, with her ankles chained to the floor, arms encased behind in a single glove, with her back arched to present her superbly firm breasts most invitingly. Her arms were pulled up by a rope attached to the end of the glove, forcing her to press herself down on the dildo and the sharp wedge that constituted the top of the horse. She was naked, her smooth, the beads of perspiration dotting her pale, pink flesh glittering like a thousand diamonds.

Halli was a lithe, beautiful girl, with a fresh, youthful perfection that Caine found most fetching. Betty Carroll was just as appealing, but in a very different way. She had a more mature, womanly body, with fuller, rounder breasts, somewhat fleshier, but still well-muscled thighs and buttocks, and more prominent, softly curving hips. In short, the Wireless Schoolteacher was a delight to the eye.

Still, she was no more so than Caine's other bed slaves. Nonetheless, she still not as beautiful as slaves Caine had grown tired of and given to Quentin, such as Elenora Riley with her incomparable breasts, or the entrancing little pixie, Inga Bergqvist. Caine did not own bed slaves who were less than stunningly attractive, so mere physical beauty hardly made an impression on him any longer.

What made *this* woman so fascinating was her unique personality, a brazen manipulator, who posed as an innocent virgin, with her smoldering sexuality just below the surface. Caine found the mental images of her begging to be used in any number of humiliating and painful ways, forcing her to come, then punishing her for doing so, training her as a cart pony and so forth, unusually arousing. In addition, although he was not consciously aware of it, he was still not comfortable with the way he had allowed Halli to decide how they would couple, even if the subsequent sex more than justified it. Caine therefore felt a greater than usual need to demonstrate to himself that he was still the master, who demanded strict obedience from his chattels and got it. For a demonstration of this sort, the amoral and faithless murderer, temptress, and cock-teasing virgin, Betty Carroll, was the ideal subject.

She asked a garbled, unintelligible question through the mouth-filling gag when he came into the room. Caine responded by walking quickly over the bound, blindfolded woman, snatching up a light dog-whip from a rack in passing, then snapping it across her back, drawing a stifled shriek. After he made a sarcastic and unjustified observation about her intelligence (whatever criticisms might be justly made about her morals, Betty was very intelligent,) he spent the next quarter-hour punishing her, beginning by slamming her in the solar plexus with a rubber truncheon. He continued from there, methodically working her over, until she slumped heavily on the horse, only half-conscious.

He put the club aside, lifted her off the horse, and pulled the dripping ball-gag out of her mouth. He then slipped a noose around her neck, pulling it close around the base of her jaw. This noose was at the end of a rope that hung down from an electrically powered spool directly over Betty's head. Caine pressed a button, the spool revolved and the rope grew taut, drawing her up on her toes. When he stopped, her constricted trachea was making a harsh, distinctly audible with each inhale and exhale.

He spoke to her while he explored her delicious body, fondling her breasts, and probing her orifices with his fingers. As he had many times before with other new chattels, he secured her compliance with threats, in this instance, strangulation. The threat was all the more effective after the sample hanging he conducted, when the nose lifted her off the floor, until her eyes bulged out and her face was deep crimson from asphyxiation.

After that, Betty offered no resistance when he excited her, once again employing his time-tested method of rubbing a powerful aphrodisiac cream into her nipples and sex, until she was frantic in her need. He brought her to the edge of an enormous orgasm, then left her hanging, paddled her when she protested, and demanded that she beg for his cock. When she did, he began to manually manipulate her anus, preparing this tiny orifice for his now-rampant erection.

Soon, the cowering Betty was kneeling on all fours before him, too afraid of Caine to move or even protest when she felt the swollen mushroom of his cock up against her rear entry. She was completely under control, his to use however he wished. This was the climactic moment, when Caine would demonstrate his control over the new slave with a long, painful buggering. Normally, this was a high point in training for, moments that kept him interested in acquiring and training new girls.

He took his cock in hand and ran it vigorously up and down through the valley between her smooth bottom globes, then stopped with the head poised against the trembling Betty's brown starburst. This was the big moment. He gritted his teeth, dug his fingers into her hips, and began to force his way into the undersized hole... then stopped.

What's the trouble, now? He demanded silently of himself. This was not a recurrence of his brief bout of impotence. Quentin had fixed that little problem for good with the gift of the two teen bluebloods, Daphne and Astrid on the occasion of his 60th birthday (see *By Judicial Decree 11: Negotiable Instrument* for their story. CJB.) In any event, one look at his cock, which felt hard enough to hammer nails, was enough to dispose of any possible doubt on the question. So, what *was* it, then?

179

"For Odin's sake!" he exclaimed in disgust, when the answer came to him. It was that pious, little Fairbourne slut, of course! She had somehow gotten into his head, and completely ruined the pleasure he should be taking from training this new slave. He rose from the floor, the submissive Betty forgotten.

How dare *that little bitch*...! He thought, his face reddening in anger. He cut the thought short, and to the lasting astonishment of the naked Wireless Schoolteacher, said, "She didn't do anything except show me I was in a rut, when I couldn't see it for myself. I've been doing the same old thing so long, I've completely forgotten that anything else is possible."

"Umm...were you addressing me, by chance, Master?" Betty asked in her smallest, most submissive tone.

"What?" Caine snapped, as if suddenly recalling that she was there. "No, no, I was just talking to myself. You'll start doing it too when get to be as old as I am, assuming you live that long. I was just advising myself that it was past time to make some changes around here."

He picked up a phone and began talking into it very rapidly. When he was done, he slammed the receiver back in the cradle decisively, looked meaningfully at Betty, and said. "This is going to be fun..., for me, I mean," he added, "if not so much for you."

***

That evening, the supervisor of Briarcliff's greensuits received an order so strange that she asked Caine to repeat it, just to make sure she had heard him aright. She, in turn, was obliged to repeat the order twice to the two house slaves assigned the duty, for precisely the same reason. All concerned having confirmed to their satisfaction that they were not suffering from some sort of shared auditory hallucination, the two greensuits proceeded to the suite assigned to the new fuck-toy, bringing with them garments selected by Master Caine himself for the occasion (Another anomaly! New fuck-toys never were permitted to have clothes so early in their training,) then escorted her to the small dining room (containing a forty-foot long ivory inlaid teak dining table and lit by an even dozen solid gold candelabras. "Small" did not necessarily mean the same thing at Briarcliff as it did elsewhere,) for a... *private dinner with Caine*!? It was unheard of, unbelievable, impossible. No one in the entire mansion, not even the ancient janitor, Sven Olsen, who had started there on the day Caine took possession of the great house, had ever heard of him inviting one of his slaves to have dinner with him. Why, it was practically a *date*!

This dinner ran directly in the face of a rule Caine had strictly enforced: slaves should act like slaves at all times, and must never forget their place. Any slave he even *suspected* of forgetting her place was severely punished. "Familiarity breeds contempt," he would tell the unfortunate chattel who had become overly familiar with himself, or indeed, with any free person in Briarcliff, whether he was one of Caine's numerous employees, or merely a visitor. Then he would start whipping her.

181

Evidently, the new girl, Halli Fairbourne was to be exempt from this rule, at least for now.

The house slaves delivered her to the dining room at 6:30 and did not return until summoned back more than four hours later. Caine and Halli spent the evening discussing her ideas and working out the details around mouthfuls of food. She was extremely creative, proposing numerous interesting bondage arrangements, many of which had never occurred to Caine before. Caine found the talk almost as exhilarating as actual slave training. In the end, after considering and rejecting her more exotic ideas as impractical, he settled on a relatively simple set-up for Halli and Betty Carroll's session the next day. It was so simple, in fact, that Caine was surprised he had not thought of it himself long before.

The following night, Quentin had his regular weekly supper with Caine. This was their "boy's night out," a purely social occasion, where conversation about business was forbidden. At these dinners they ate, talked, smoked post-prandial cigars, sipped French brandy, and toyed with the delicious bodies of whichever pair of his bed-slaves Caine had selected to wait on them. Quentin always appreciated these opportunities to renew his acquaintance with girls he had purchased for Caine, but rarely or never had a chance to tease, spank, arouse, or otherwise play with them, except at these weekly meals.

He was even more pleased than usual by the waitress Caine had assigned to him on this particular night, the slender, graceful Khalistani,

Serani Bohkur. She had been charged with treason and sentenced to enslavement by the Sultan Mehmet IV of Khalistan (in fact her real crime was being the daughter of a politician who had publicly criticized the Sultan's tyranny,) and given by him to Caine as a gift. Quentin had brought her home, and during the long journey from Khalistan had contrived to form a crush on the lovely, responsive, and affectionate Serani. (More about Serani's misfortunes and many other things can be found in *By Judicial Decree 10: A Case of Libel*. CJB.) Quentin had only seen her in passing a few times since he had turned her over to Caine's nonexistent mercies, and each brief encounter had only intensified his desire to spend some time with her.

After the dessert dishes had been cleared away, Quentin had summoned Serani over to sit in his lap. He thought she was more exciting than ever in the scandalous "French maid" outfit provided by Caine, which, starting at the bottom, consisted of white stiletto high heels, white mid-thigh silk stockings, a tiny white lace apron, white cloth neckband and a ridiculous little lace cap. Other than that, there was only a silver chain belt around the waist, leather cuffs (white, naturally) on the wrists and ankles that were attached by more chains to the belt, and a matching white ball gag. The chains were adjustable, allowing the waitresses to be restrained in any number of interesting positions.

Quentin took full advantage of this last feature. He had drawn Serani's hands and feet close together behind her back, then bent her over his lap to finger her sex until she squirmed with excitement, pleaded

183

for him to either stop or rub more vigorously (the ball gag made her exact words a matter for speculation.)

Whatever the young Khalistani beauty had been attempting to convey when Quentin *began* to fondle her intimately, after a very few minutes of this treatment (aided, it should be noted, by the judicious application of Caine's notorious contact aphrodisiac to her labia, clitoris, nipples and anus,) both the restricted movements of her remarkably flexible body, and the limited repertoire of sounds she could make, were unmistakably telling the same story: Serani wanted Quentin to fuck her, and the sooner he did, the better she would like it.

Quentin was not in the least averse to this program. To the contrary, his organ was in a state of full readiness, and it is likely that had this dinner occurred a half-dozen years earlier, this is precisely what Quentin would have been doing at that moment.

But a long association with Caine had changed Quentin in certain ways, most profoundly in his sexual habits. At one time a man of quite conventional sexual practices and interests, Quentin had over time inevitably been influenced by Caine's powerful personality, and he now shared much of the latter's opinion that restraining, flagellating and dominating beautiful women were an essential prelude to truly satisfying copulation (although unlike Caine, Quentin derived no pleasure from hurting and humiliating his partners, nor could he bring himself to truly *hurt* them; for him, the bondage was only pleasurable in a sexual context.)

After bringing Serani to the brink of a climax twice, then stopping to administer a vigorous spanking before he resumed stroking and teasing her bulging clit and swollen labia, he judged that Serani was as excited as possible. In addition, he felt as if his testicles were on the verge of a rupture from a withheld flood of cum, so he had e removed his trousers, and was preparing to bury his rod to the root in Serani's pussy.

The inflamed head of his organ was poised on over the girl's gleaming, lubricated lips, when Caine spoke. He had chosen to be served by one of his current favorites, a direct descendant of one of the first European settlers in the Western Hemisphere, the proud, copper-haired aristocrat, Astrid Edmundson, of *the* Edmundsons. Astrid's hands were confined at her waist, kneeling at Caine's feet, being throat-fucked by her owner. Caine pushed Astrid back, and she toppled to the floor, gasping like a newly-boated trout. Caine did not even glance at her. "I well understand your desire to fuck the brains out of that little whore, Quentin," he said, "but I suggest you put it off for another time. I promise to make it up to you. You can have her tomorrow, if you like."

Quentin turned to stare at him in disbelief. "May I ask why, Mr. Caine?" he said, posing this question in a normal voice, a masterly demonstration of self-control, considering the almost overpowering impulse to shriek like a madman that *he was almost in her*!

"I have something special laid on for us tonight, and when you get there, you'll understand," Caine answered. "As unlikely as it may seem at the moment, when you see what I have arranged, you will agree that it was the right decision."

Quentin doubted it. He lowered his head to hide the expression on his face from Caine, and through clenched teeth said, "If you say so, Mr. Caine."

"Now, don't be that way, my boy," Caine said, rising and pulling up his pants. "I don't want you to feel *too* embarrassed when you have to apologize and admit I was right. Come on." Still skeptical, Quentin resumed his trousers, and followed Caine out the door.

They walked through the halls of Briarcliff to Caine's private quarters, the sulking Quentin lagging behind. "Come *along* Quentin," Caine said, with his hand on the doorknob, until the other man caught up. "They've been waiting for us in the playroom for..." he pulled a watch from his jacket, glanced at it, and finished, "...almost three hours."

The "playroom" was a smaller version of the basement dungeons conveniently located next to Caine's bedroom. It contained fewer restraints and instruments than the downstairs facilities, but still had a choice of frames, pillories and the like, over a dozen canes, whips, belts and paddles, and two or three modern electric training devices Caine was testing for the manufacturers.

Quentin entered the room behind Caine, then stopped as suddenly as if he had run into wall when he saw *who* had been kept waiting for such an unreasonable length of time. Posed intimately together atop a metal table were the two slaves Quentin had brought home from the prison sale in

186

Westmark: Halli Fairbourne and Betty Carroll. After one look, he realized that Caine had not been exaggerating about this special arrangement. Serani Bokhur could wait.

They were lying head to foot, their nude bodies bound so closely together that they almost looked like some kind of double-ended sex creature, possibly the product of a mad scientist. Halli was on top with her face buried in the wireless Schoolteacher's crotch. Her arms were drawn down under the table and bound there by some means that was invisible to Quentin. Halli was kneeling over Betty's face, her sex hovering so close to the former's mouth that her pale pubic hairs were brushing her partner's lips. She was fixed in this position by leather straps that secured her lower legs to the tabletop, straps pulled so tightly that the flesh of her calves bulged out between them.

Betty was tied up in a way that might possibly have been even more uncomfortable. A strap around her throat kept her head pinned back to the table. She was laying on top of her arms, which were tied wrist to wrist and elbow to elbow. This forced her to arch up, lifting her luscious buttocks clear of the table. Her upper and lower legs were doubled up and bound together with uncompromising strictness, her thighs were spread wide, as if in welcome, and her sex and asshole were raised at an ideal angle, as if she was a display mannequin in the window of the world's most expensive whorehouse. In short, Betty appeared to be positively *begging* to be ravished.

The slaves were blindfolded, their eyes hidden under layers of cloth tape. In addition, their mouths had been reduced to cock receptacles by ring gags that pried their jaws agonizingly wide apart. Altogether, the composition was very nearly enough to make Quentin explode before he laid a finger on them.

"Well," Caine said, gesturing at the display, "what do you think, my boy? Now that you've seen my little surprise, if you still want to fuck the Khalistani slut instead, it's not too late." He turned to look at Serani and Astrid, who had followed them from the dining hall.

Quentin did not even trouble himself to reply to this suggestion. "It's...I mean, they're...umm...well..." he stuttered. "I've never seen bondage like this before. I assume it's something new. How did you happen to think of it?"

Caine went over to the table, reached between Halli's thighs and Betty's mouth to cup the former's mound in his hand, and said, "Why, I *didn't* think of it. Our girl here came up with just about the whole thing by herself." As he spoke the words "our girl," Caine rammed his first two fingers and thumb up her anus, making her lurch and cry out in surprise and pain. "Didn't you?" he demanded, plunging the invading digits violently in and out of her rectum, stretching and distorting the delicate orifice.

Halli neither affirmed nor denied it, unless her bellowed "Harrr!" or the gush of accumulated saliva from her gaping jaws was one or the other. She made more unintelligible sounds when Caine

188

continued probing of her narrow passage, accompanying her muffled outcries by violently flinging her lower body about, and unintentionally knocking around the unfortunate Betty, batting her head back and forth with her thighs.

Caine popped his fingers out, then shoved them into Betty's mouth, which was conveniently located just below, and growling, "Lick me clean, cunt," which she did promptly. As Betty was washing the residue of the interior of her partner's colon from his hand, Caine turned to Quentin, and said, "I'd like to fuck Halli first, then come in the other cunt's mouth, while you're doing her at the other end. Then, after we rest up a bit, we can switch around. How does that sound, my boy?"

"It sounds remarkably generous of you, Mr. Caine, even more than usual," Quentin answered. He looked longingly at the nude, helpless Betty, then added, "But are you quite certain? I mean, these are both brand new slaves, and Betty was a virgin until yesterday..."

"And she still is," Caine interrupted. "I didn't pop her cork yesterday. Her cherry is all yours."

" But Mr. Caine," Quentin protested, "she's your slave, and it wouldn't be right..."

"Nonsense, Quentin," Caine told him. "Consider it an early birthday present, if that will make it easier for you." When the other man still hesitated, Caine went on, "If you reject my gift, I will take it as a personal slight." He frowned to show he was serious.

"In that case, I don't see that I have any choice in the matter," Quentin said. He bowed and said,

"Once again, you have added to a debt I can never repay, Mr. Caine. I don't know what I did to deserve such generosity, but I want you to know how grateful I am for everything that you have given me, especially the four women I love."

"You have earned, every farthing and every girl," Caine assured him. "Now why don't we try to forget about what a wonderful fellow I am for a little while, and start fucking these whores?" Suiting his deeds to his words, he unbuttoned his pants, stepped out of them, and presented the turgid shaft of his cock to Halli's lower lips, flopping his scrotum on Betty's upturned face.

He grabbed a handful of the latter's hair, yanked her head sharply back, and commanded, "Suck my balls, bitch." She did not hesitate, drawing the wrinkled bag of flesh into her mouth, and carefully washing it with her tongue. *This one's thoroughly broken already*, he thought, a little disappointed. He had hoped that the virginal, man-hating Wireless Schoolteacher would have put up a better fight. Aloud he remarked, "They don't make 'em like they used to, do they?"

Quentin had been fondling Betty's pussy, applying Caine's aphrodisiac cream where it would do the most good, and watching her hips writhe under his fingers. He looked up. "I'm sorry, Mr. Caine," he said. "I'm afraid I wasn't paying attention. Could you repeat that?"

Caine had his cock in his hand and was working it up and down just inside Halli's engorged sex lips, gathering greasy lubrication on the head. "Don't stop licking me, slut," he muttered to Betty,

190

as he pulled out of Halli's pussy, relocating the head of his rod to the brown star of her anus. To Quentin, he replied, "It was just an old man talking to himself, my boy; nothing that need concern you."

"This should be good for a few centuries off from your stay in the Dark Place, I imagine," Caine told Halli. He pressed his hips in, driving his cock home with the full force of his body. Displayed with her legs wide apart as she was, she was helpless to resist Caine's well-lubricated invader. He opened the way through the delicate portal to her bowels with ease, and all Halli could do was lie there and endure the terrible sensation of his cock stretching her anal ring to three times normal diameter. She stopped what she had been doing (she had been polishing the shaft of Quentin's erection with her tongue,) lifted her head and shrieked as if she was already suffering the torments of the afterlife.

Caine crammed more of his meat into her colon, obliging her poor rectum to conform to the barrel of his organ, and remarked, "You'll soon learn to enjoy this, if I'm any judge of your sexual capacities. Most of them do, you know." He paused, with half his length buried in the screaming girl's back passage. "Which makes me wonder: will you still get time off in Hell for being ass-fucked, if you're getting pleasure from it? An interesting question, don't you agree? I would be surprised if the Book of Life deals with that specific situation."

Halli's reply, a bellowed "*Ahhhh!*" was ambiguous at best. Caine decided that she might be too distracted to discuss the matter intelligently at that moment. There would be time enough to debate

191

theology later. He shrugged. *Live in the moment*, he told himself. He took a firmer grip on her hips, jammed the final inches of his cock into her bottomhole, growled, "Now *fuck* me, you little cunt!" and began pumping her in earnest.

Had he been given the choice, Quentin would have preferred to copulate with Halli, but Betty Carroll was hardly a booby prize. She had a wonderfully firm body. The flesh of her bottom and thighs was as smooth as any he had ever handled, her pussy had only the lightest garnish of delicate, curling hairs (he found thick pubic jungles unattractive) that did nothing to conceal the slightly pouting, pink lips of her sex, while the pinkish-brown asterisk of her anus seemed to be winking at him, as if in welcome. Moreover, Betty was a virgin, which Quentin had never been offered before. There was something about a defloration that gave the sexual act an extra thrill, especially when the virgin was as desirable as the one bound naked and defenseless beneath him. The fact that she was a pretty poor example of a human being, being a liar, murderer and sociopath, who would have been beheaded by the state for her crimes, had she committed them here in Karlsvania, relieved Quentin's usually sensitive conscience. He would not be troubled by guilt over anything he did to Betty Carroll.

However, the thought of being the first to sodomize that trim behind was at least as attractive as a traditional defloration. "Are you ready, Miss Carroll?" he asked, scooping goo from her slot with his fingers, rubbing it around the entrance to her colon, then working it inside, stretching the little hole in preparation for his cock. "I'm going to start back here."

With her mouth full of Caine's testicles, it was quite impossible for Betty to explain that she was very much *not* ready, and furthermore, that she would *never* be ready to have a cock shoved up her ass. The best she could manage was a mumbled and quite incomprehensible protest that sounded like "Uummppff! Mmmuuh." This earned her a "Good girl!" from Caine, who found her efforts to speak generated delightful vibrations on his sack, but it did not win her a reprieve from Quentin, nor even a delay.

"Good," Quentin said, "then let's begin, shall we?" With the head of his rod resting on her brown sunburst, he dug his thumbs into the inner surfaces of her bottom cheeks and pulled them wide, while pressing down with his hips. Betty had been desperately preparing to resist, squeezing the powerful muscles surrounding her little hole with all her might. She had not considered the possibility that he might separate her buttocks in this fashion, and she screeched in surprise when the blunt head of Quentin's cock gained purchase inside her, penetrating a half-inch.

Betty panicked. She spat out Caine's scrotum, flung her head to the side, and screamed, "No! Stop it!" with all the power in her lungs. Since she was still hampered by the ring gag, this emerged as "Uhhhh! Ahhh-ehh!" She would have continued in this vein, but for Caine's intervention. He clamped his big hand around her throat then squeezed until she was making a gurgling sound, and her face had turned dark red from lack of air.

"Who the *fuck* gave you permission to stop licking me?" Caine demanded in a voice of iron. "I thought you wanted to continue your worthless existence as a fuck toy. Have you changed your mind?"

She shook her head, turning it blindly in his direction him.

"No?" he asked. "Then you had better show me you mean it, *right now*. Because if you haven't convinced me in the next thirty seconds that you want to be pleasure slave..., a *live* pleasure slave," he added, "as soon as I finish fucking you, or possibly *while* I'm doing it, I will dispense with your services...permanently. Do I make myself plain?" He released her throat, leaving red fingermarks on the white flesh.

"*Ehh! Ehh!*" Betty exclaimed hoarsely, nodding her head violently. Before Caine could give the order aloud, she extended her neck to recapture his testicles in her mouth, then resumed massaging them with her tongue. Caine gave her one, long sidelong glance, then went back to ferociously buggering Halli. After that, Betty concentrated her entire being on giving Caine as much pleasure as possible from a tongue washing. While her body twisted in agony from the rough way Quentin plundered her bottomhole, she did not move her head more than an inch, other than to follow when Caine shifted his position. Even after he came, ramming every millimeter of his cock deep into Halli's colon, and pulled out, she continued to try to

194

lick him, reaching out desperately with her tongue to demonstrate her sincere desire to serve.

She felt a great sense of relief, when Caine ordered her to clean his cock in her mouth, for she took this as an indication that he had found her service acceptable. She cheerfully, even eagerly, swallowed his semi-hard organ, offering no protest or resistance of any kind when he drove into her throat, making her gag, and cutting off her air. If he approved of her efforts, she reasoned, he would not kill her...probably.

Betty suffered momentary doubts about this theory, when dark spots caused by anoxia started to dance before her dimming eyes. But before she dropped off into the Big Sleep, Caine came out, allowing her to gasp enough oxygen in time to stave off unconsciousness. After that, her head flopped back on the table, where she remained, silent and motionless during the long buggering by Quentin. When he finally came, his cock pulsing deep inside her belly, she sighed in relief.

The relief did not last very long. While the men recuperated, withdrawing to comfortable chairs and sipping drinks brought by the waitresses, the two women on the table were put back to work exciting each other with for the entertainment of their masters. Although her tongue was becoming limp from the unusual exertion, Betty uncomplainingly resumed flicking the clitoris before her until it grew erect again, rubbing her lips over the rubbery nub, then scraping it gently with her teeth and doing anything else she could think of to arouse Halli and satisfy the Master. (After her near-death experience at his hands, Betty had begun to think of Caine this way, including the capital "M.")

Halli was likewise doing her best to ignore the throbbing of her much-abused anus and the exciting things Betty's tongue was doing to her, to concentrate on licking and sucking Betty's goo-filled sex. She could tell by the way the other woman's hips rose to meet her that she was succeeding. As the wave of arousal rose and peaked, Halli became less and less inhibited, until she found herself nose deep in Betty's pussy, screaming something unclear even to herself, when she sprayed her partner's face with cum as she shuddered through another big climax. Betty followed soon after, clutching Halli's head in her thighs, and squirting fishy fluid all over the girl's pretty face.

The two men watched transfixed by the orgasms of the intertwined naked, writhing women. "This makes me think of setting up something like this with Jo Langstrom," Caine remarked. "If these two hetro bitches can make rug munching this hot, just think what a real lesbo like the Colonel could do. It would be the highlight of any movie it was in."

Quentin, like Caine, kept his eyes locked on the women. "Who would you pair her with?" he asked. "Marja, perhaps? They'd be very photogenic."

"Perhaps," Caine answered. "I'll have to think about it. Meanwhile," he said, glancing at the other man's renewed erection, "you look ready for another round, and I want a crack at the schoolmarm. Thank you for saving her maidenhead for me. You really didn't need to do that, you know." He rose, and went around behind Betty.

Quentin copied him, rising and positioning himself with his cock lightly brushing Halli's nether lips. "It was quite literally my pleasure, Mr. Caine," he said. "I didn't give up anything. Her ass was superb; she squeezed me like a tube of toothpaste."

"Let's see how ready you are for another ride," Caine told Betty. He fingered her pussy and clit, rubbing in another dose of sex cream, then spread a bit on her anus as well. In less than a minute, she was panting and arching up eagerly to meet his questing fingers. Before two minutes had passed, her hips were being led around by Caine's fingers, and she was inarticulately pleading for him to enter her.

Caine smiled, and pulled his hand away. "I didn't quite get that, my dear," he said. "Would you kindly repeat it?"

"*Eeee uuuch gee! Ahh eeeh ohhh ooo gee acheh!*" she cried, desperately trying to articulate her meaning while wearing a ring gag that made the production of the necessary consonants impossible. Caine, of course, had no trouble deciphering her meaning, which was: "Please fuck me! I beg you to fuck me, Master!"

He held his cock in his hand, then pressed it against the swollen pink lips of her sex. When she moaned and thrust her hips out to engulf him, he pulled away again. "If you're *sure* you want me to fuck you…" he waited for her to confirm it, which she did by nodding and making a tormented, desperate cry of "*Ehhh!*," before he continued,

"...then you will do *nothing* without instructions from me. *I* will direct you, and we will proceed according to the pace set by *me*. Savvy?"

Once again, she nodded.

"Right," he said. He slowly parted the outer lips of her pussy with the fat helmet on the tip of his rod, then with equal care, penetrated the inner lips as well. Betty's entire body trembled from the effort of controlling herself against the ancient urges that commanded her to fill the aching void of her sex by impaling herself on his cock.

"While we're here, perhaps you can answer a few questions about your career as a juvenile criminal," Caine suggested. As he spoke, he painstakingly inserted another inch of his cock into Betty's slot, who moaned and made tiny motions with her hips. Caine judged these to be involuntary, and after a moment's reflection, decided to refrain from correcting her for disobedience.

"Ehhh uhhh," Betty replied, which Caine understood to mean "Yes, sir."

Caine now began to move his hips in a series of tiny thrusts, each one going a little deeper, then stopping when he encountered the bit of flesh that guarded her maidenhood. As he had intended, this process aroused the already over-stimulated and under-satisfied Betty to the point of insanity. She made a wordless sound, like a walrus giving birth, and trembled more violently than ever.

Caine didn't seem to notice. "What I would like to know is this: out of all those times when you were in bed with men, didn't you ever have the urge to let one of them fuck you?" he asked. "Weren't you curious about sex?"

This time, her gape-mouthed answer was so garbled, that not even he could make any sense of it. He grunted in annoyance and said, "Oh Quentin, could you kindly take out the Schoolmarm's gag? I'm trying to have a conversation, and ..."

"Yes, of course, Mr. Caine," Quentin said, taking a moment from fucking Halli to release the strap behind Betty's head, and removing the saliva-coated ring from her mouth. The latter worked her jaw from side to side, trying to revive the muscles that had been forced unnaturally wide for hours, so she could speak.

While he waited for Betty to regain the power of speech, he resumed fucking her, now moving his cock back until only the head was inside her, then returning to probe a fraction of an inch deeper with each leisurely thrust. This served to heat Betty up until she thought the top of her head might blow off if he did not fill her pussy with his fat tool instantly.

"Gods above!" she cried. "Master, I beg you, fuck me or kill me, I don't care which!" She arched up in a mad effort to capture his cock in her ravenous slot.

"Answer my questions," Caine responded, backing off again, "and maybe I will."

"Ahh...ahh.." she panted, "what was...it? I've... I've forgotten what you asked me."

Caine shook his head. "I can't see how anyone with as poor a memory as you was allowed to teach..." He stopped. "I asked if you ever had any interest in sex back in the days when you were

199

working that blackmail scheme with your late partner. Well, did you?"

Betty closed her eyes and tried to think through the thick fog of lust that had settled over her brain. "I...no, no...I despised those...men, all men. Lars...was always trying to..." then suddenly interrupted herself to scream, "For the love of Odin, Master Caine, *please*!"

Caine frowned. "You cunts today have absolutely no self-control," he grumbled. With obvious reluctance, he said "All right, I'll give you a good reaming, but if you come without permission, you'll be punished for insubordination. Do we have a deal?" He asked.

At that moment she would have agreed to anything. As it happened, she was too excited to make sense of anything he said after "all right," and was not actually aware of the terms. She shrieked, "Yes! Yes! Whatever you say! Just *do it*!"

"Hmmph," he grunted, sinking his fingers into the flesh of her hips, "what's the big hurry? You're going to be a fuck-toy for another 10 or 15 years, at least..." he chose this moment to ram the remaining eight inches of his erection into her pussy, ripping through her hymen and not stopping until he felt the head bottoming out against the entrance to her cervix.

Betty threw her head back and screamed wordlessly, her hips bucking wildly under Caine. The soft walls of her pussy gripped his cock in a madness of pleasure that went on for what seemed like an eternity to Betty. When it was over, she lay limp and boneless under Halli, her all-consuming need finally satisfied. She was at peace with the world.

Then Caine spoke. "I warned you not to come without permission," he said coldly. "Instead of going to bed tonight, you will be spending eight hours down in Room One with a little gadget called the CliMaxer, and after that, perhaps, you will learn not to indulge yourself by disobeying my orders."

"I…I'm sorry Master," Betty blurted, "but I just couldn't help my-…"

"On the CliMaxer, you will enjoy six enforced orgasms per hour," he continued as if she had not spoken, "and you will do so until, in my opinion, the lesson has been learned."

Betty thought about what an entire night of forced orgasms would be like, and immediately started to plead for mercy and promise to be perfectly obedient, if he gave her another chance. Caine ignored her. He picked up a telephone and started to speak into it, then stopped, put his hand over the mouthpiece and said, "Quentin, could you do something about that racket? I can't hear myself think."

"Right away, Mr. Caine," he answered. He reinstalled Betty's gag, overcoming her resistance by pinching her nose shut when she refused to voluntarily open her mouth, then muted her cries by sealing the ring with a thick, five-inch long dildo.

"That's much better," Caine said. He nodded and returned to his call. A few minutes later, a pair of green-uniformed house servants came to take Betty away. "I'll drop by to see how you are getting along after breakfast tomorrow," Caine called after her.

Betty had imagined that 8 hours on Caine's CliMaxer would be as bad as the strangulation she had endured on the first day, which was the most terrible experience of her life. As it turned out, she was wrong. It was worse.

Chapter Thirteen: In the Barn

Two weeks later, Caine and Quentin were having breakfast together. As Quentin was finishing his final cup of tea, Caine said, "I'm going over to the stables from here. I'd like you to come with me, if you're not busy." Caine had a stable, indoor riding ring and outdoor track where he trained his bed slaves as draft animals, to keep them in top physical condition. Also, he loved to humiliate them and to hear their sweet cries when he made them pull him in a sulky or dogcart with well-aimed strokes of his whip.

Quentin drained the last of the Orange Pekoe from his cup, patted his mouth with a napkin, pushed back his chair and came to his feet. Although he had planned to start in the enormous annual task of preparing the tax returns for Caine Enterprises that morning, he was able to answer quite truthfully, "Not at all, Mr. Caine." This was because he had long ago decided that he would *always* be available for Caine, no matter what else he was doing

The stables were a pleasant fifteen minute walk from the mansion. As they strode along in the crisp late autumn air, Caine said casually, "Last night, I offered to free Halli and hire her to devise bondages for the studio and my personal enjoyment."

Quentin stopped in his tracks to study the other man's face, trying to decide if Caine was pulling his leg. "Mr. Caine," he said, "you wouldn't be taking advantage of poor, stupid, Quentin's gullibility again, would you sir?"

Caine shook his head and resumed walking. "It's no joke, my boy," he said. "Halli has a positive genius for the work, and I felt certain she would be more creative if she was a free citizen." He paused, and looking a little uncomfortable, Quentin thought, added "Also, I have very quickly grown …hrumm…" he cleared his throat, as if reluctant to admit it, and finished, "…fond of her."

Quentin was shocked into speechlessness by this revelation. He peeked sidelong at the man walking at his side. Could Caine, notorious for his cruel mistreatment of even the gentlest, most obedient girls, have developed a schoolboy crush on a…l, a *schoolgirl*? Could he be in… *love*?

They were both silent until they reached the top of the hill where the stables were located. By then Quentin had recovered enough to speak. "So?" he asked. "What was her answer, Mr. Caine? I assume she said yes."

Caine did not answer immediately. He continued into the barn where the girls were housed when they did pony service, followed closely by Quentin. He stopped before one stall, and waited until Quentin stood at his side, and they could both see the occupant of the stall. "No," Caine said sadly, "she turned me down." Standing in the dark stall, shivering, in the cool late autumn air and naked but for a halter and a thick wooden bit, was the beautiful, young Halli Fairbourne.

***

204

Caine seized Halli by the lead clipped to the halter strapped around her head, drew her out of her stall, and lead her to the big tack room where the carts were stored.. He tied the lead to a post and left her there while he selected a vehicle. Halli's arms were strapped behind her back at the wrist and elbow, the latter so strictly that they touched, obliging her to adopt an exaggerated, upright, chest-out posture that displayed her breasts spectacularly.

"Why?" Quentin whispered to her while Caine was out of earshot. "Why didn't you take the deal, Halli?"

She answered, but with the bit severely restricting her use of her tongue and lips, all that came from her mouth were nonsense syllables: "Aghh eeh oooh uhh..." and some accumulated drool. The latter flooded over her chin, to drip down on her breasts and belly. She rolled her eyes and stamped her foot, frustrated by her inability to speak coherently.

Caine returned, drawing a racing sulky, a lightly built, aluminum two-wheeled cart, behind him. He put Halli between the shafts and began to hitch her up. As he did, he said, "You asked her why she turned me down while I was fetching the sulky, didn't you, Quentin?" Without waiting for an answer, he went on, "It was her religion, you see. She didn't believe she would suffer sufficiently as a freedwoman, and of course that would mean, oh, centuries and centuries more time in ...what do you call it..., ah yes, the *Dark Place*." He enunciated the final two words with sarcastic precision. "So, she *had* to say no, you see."

It was plain that Halli had not foreseen how deeply her rejection would offend Caine. Tears sprang into her eyes, as she tried to explain that she had never meant to hurt him, that she loved him as a man and respected him as her Master. Once again, her words were reduced to gibberish.

Caine rounded on her and slapped her ringingly with an open hand. "Ponies do not speak," he said. His voice now was as cold as a glacier, his face set and expressionless. "If you cannot control your tongue, I can easily have it removed." Halli shuddered and looked away, unable to meet his eyes.

Caine settled himself into the seat of the sulky, holding a short whip in one hand and the reins, which were harnessed to the Halli's nipples with toothed spring-clips, in the other. He shook the reins, making Halli's breasts bob enticingly, drawing a yelp from the draft animal.

"*Hup*, pony," he called, nipping her hindquarters with a flick of the whip, and making her cry out again. "Step lively, now. You're taking me to the dairy today, and you'll do it at a trot." The dairy was in a distant part of the estate, over five miles of hilly terrain.

Halli trotted out the open gate, then was halted by Caine, who pulled back sharply on the reins. He turned and called back to Quentin. "Ah, I almost forgot why I asked you to come out here with me, Quentin. I had Betty put in Stall #3 last night, because I want to start her pony training as well. I'd like you to break her to harness while I'm working with Halli."

206

"Yes, sir, Mr. Caine," Quentin said. "I'll take care of it right away." He took one more look at the weeping girl pulling Caine's cart, shook his head, then turned to walk back into the barn.

The End

"Yes, sir, Mr. Cainer," Quentin said. "I'll take care of it right away." He took one more look at the weeping girl pulling Caine's cart, shook his head then turned to walk back into the barn.

The End

CPSIA information can be obtained
at www.ICGtesting.com
Printed in the USA
LVHW042034210921
698348LV00005B/234

9 781786 955982